"Just so you know, I know two models who ended their...careers early because they got cocky and tried to steal from me."

Her breath caught in her throat. Her ears were ringing. She was pretty sure he was talking about what had happened to Gena and Bianca. Vanessa swallowed hard. Her eyes widened as she realized that her shaking fingers were actually stroking the gun beneath the covers.

Angry as hell, she saw herself fitting the smooth metal into the palm of her hand, lifting the barrel with the aim and precision that won her awards, and hitting him right between the eyes. Lord knew she wanted to do it. It was the least she could do for Gena and Bianca.

Dear Reader,

I was excited to get the opportunity to write Vanessa Dawson's story, *A Model Spy,* in Silhouette Bombshell's THE IT GIRLS continuity. Tough, yet beautiful and vulnerable, Vanessa Dawson kicks butt and tries to deal with her family, an evolving relationship and past demons returning to haunt her. For me, this effort represents a significant departure from the traditional idea of a series book as far as tone and content, while also incorporating a strong, competent heroine who is an African-American heiress and ex-supermodel.

The groundbreaking doesn't stop there, either. My heroine has past issues that affect her ability to do her assignment and she gets to choose her hero from a sexy DEA agent and a handsome hip-hop music mogul who came up from the Miami street gangs, not unlike people you find in the news today. I enjoyed listening to the hip-hop music and reading about the roads the artists traveled to fame and fortune and the problems many face. I hope I managed to impart a little of that flavor in this book.

Natalie Dunbar

A MODEL SPY

NATALIE DUNBAR

THE IT GIRLS

BOMBSHELL™

Published by Silhouette Books

America's Publisher of Contemporary Romance

Special thanks and acknowledgment are given
to Natalie Dunbar for her contribution to THE IT GIRLS.

SILHOUETTE BOOKS

ISBN 0-373-51388-7

A MODEL SPY

www.SilhouetteBombshell.com

Printed in U.S.A.

Books by Natalie Dunbar

Silhouette Bombshell

Private Agenda #15
*A Model Spy #74

*The It Girls

NATALIE DUNBAR

believes that a woman can do anything she sets her mind to. To date she has met her personal goals of becoming an electrical engineer working in the field, obtaining her master's degree in business administration and getting published. Happily married to her high school sweetheart, she lives in the Detroit area with him and their two boys. She has several romance novels under her belt, and is ecstatic over the launch of Silhouette Bombshell, which gives her characters new worlds to conquer. An avid fan of fiction, television and movies that showcase powerful women with strong skills and talents in a male-dominated world, she is happy to add her heroines, CIA agent Reese Whittaker and model-spy Vanessa Dawson, to the list.

I'd like to dedicate this book to my wonderful family.
Thanks for all your love and support!
Natalie

Acknowledgments:

Thanks to my wonderful editor, Julie Barrett, for great ideas and help in shaping this book to make it the best. Thanks to my husband, Chet, for inspiration, input and just listening. Thanks to my youngest son, for doing without Mom when there was no other way. I want to thank my critique group, specifically Karen and Reon for all their help and support. Special thanks to Joe Kilmer in the DEA Miami Field Office (MFO) and the DEA Web site, http://www.usdoj.gov/dea/. Any errors in how the process works are mine.

Prologue

"Renee, are you available? There's a call for you on the private line in your office."

Olivia's voice drew Renee's attention away from the limousine taking off from the front of the town house to enter the 68th Street traffic. It was carrying her husband, Preston, and her daughter, Haley, to a matinee.

With Preston newly released from prison, it should have been the best of times for her family, but the man who'd come home a few months ago was a pale shadow of the one who'd left. Worse yet,

she barely recognized Haley, who'd recently transformed into an angry, rebellious teen.

Renee promised herself that she would hold her
family together and make things right, but now, she
had a job to do.

With an incline of her auburn head and murmured
thanks to her personal assistant, Renee Dalton Sinclair crossed the Persian rug and passed the spiral
stairs on the first floor of The Gotham Rose Club to
head back to her office. Nervous excitement made
the back of her neck itch. The only person who ever
called on her private line was the Governess, a mysterious benefactress who was well placed in the government. Whenever the calls came, one of the
Gotham Rose's undercover spies soon took on a
dangerous mission to bring down a high-society
criminal.

Whoever the Governess was, she'd been powerful enough to pull the strings necessary to have
Renee's beloved husband, Preston, released from
prison early. Despite Pres's refusal to discuss what
had happened, she knew he had been the scapegoat
for his corrupt family and their investment firm.

The Governess had approached Renee four years
ago with a deal. In return for Pres's early release,
Renee started an undercover organization with her
exclusive Gotham Rose women's club. Renee had

started the club to get New York's wealthiest young heiresses to put their names and fortunes to good use by raising money for charity. The secret spy club included only a small number of the more than two hundred Gotham Rose members. The women were trained to take down upper-class citizens who used wealth and power to cover their crimes.

In the quiet sanctuary of her office, Renee secured the door, then slipped into her powder room and locked that door too. Making herself comfortable on the overstuffed, white love seat, she lifted the receiver from the vanity table.

"This is Renee Dalton Sinclair."

"Renee... I trust you're enjoying Pres's return?" the mechanically distorted voice began.

Renee was overjoyed to have her husband back, but the sound of his name spoken by the disembodied voice sent chills through her. Was there a threat lurking beneath the Governess's question?

"I love my husband," she answered simply, her tone ringing with conviction. "Having him home has brought the life back to our house." In the ensuing silence she added, "Of course, I'm grateful for everything you've done—"

"Preston Sinclair was innocent," the Governess cut in. "Now let's move on to the business at hand. Have you seen the story in the papers about the two models who were killed in their Miami apartments? Another model was caught at Miami International yesterday, trying to smuggle heroin in a case of bubble bath."

"I saw the stories," Renee confirmed. "You'd think that fashion models would have more options than the poor desperate souls who normally end up being mules in the drug trade."

The Governess expelled a contemptuous puff of air. "Someone made those models an offer they couldn't refuse. We need to identify this drug ring, find out who's at the top, get the evidence and take them down fast."

Shifting the phone and its cord, Renee used her key to open a drawer at the carved antique vanity and remove the large file containing pictures and press information on all the Gotham Roses. Some of the women were just members of her charitable organization, which required all its members to pay twenty-five thousand dollars to join, ten thousand a year thereafter, and then asked that they help raise at least one hundred thousand dollars annually. She knew by heart which members were also a part of her undercover organization. They were the best, the brightest and the most capable women imaginable.

"We need someone who can move in the modeling world without raising suspicion," she murmured, paging past several members. "Someone they would actually welcome."

"We also need a high-profile, well-connected operative who can take care of herself. Vanessa Dawson would be ideal," the Governess said firmly. "We've arranged for her to get a contract with *Inside Sports* magazine for the Fantasy Swimsuit edition."

Finding Vanessa's gorgeous picture and press information in the stack, Renee shook her head. "Vanessa left the modeling world under less than ideal circumstances," she said. "It would take a lot to get her back into that life."

"The stakes are high," the Governess insisted. "Lives have been lost. The murdered models moved in circles that include some of the younger members of the old-money set. What if there is a connection between their money and the models acting as mules for the drug trade?"

What, indeed? As an heiress and bona fide member of the old-money class, nothing surprised Renee anymore. Bored people with more money than they knew what to do with were unpredictable. Renee closed her file, already imagining Vanessa back in the wild, unpredictable world she'd barely escaped. She knew Vanessa could successfully complete the assignment—but at what cost?

Chapter 1

In the secret basement training room at the Gotham Rose Club, mirrored walls surrounded a hardwood floor dotted with mats. Covered with protective gear beneath her loose, white workout *gi*, Vanessa Dawson flicked back her highlighted ponytail and aimed a long-legged side kick at trainer Jimmy Valentine.

He blocked it with a padded, muscular forearm. "Good kick, Vanessa, but we know your kicks are always good. Move in and throw some punches."

Vanessa hadn't planned to spar with Jimmy. She'd arrived early to work off a little frustration and excitement before her scheduled tea with Renee. Once Jimmy had spotted her at the abdominal machine, he'd refused to take no for an answer. She'd been long overdue for a training session. Now here she was sparring with the master of several martial arts forms, while she tried to preserve her fresh manicure.

Knees slightly bent, Vanessa crouched in a ready position. Tonight, she, Madison Taylor Pruitt and Tatiana Guttmann were going out for dinner and a night on the town. That meant she would not have time to sit through another manicure. Wrinkling her nose and lifting her arms, she balled her hands into fists and curled the thumbs underneath. Her fists flew, connecting with his protected forearms more often than she liked.

Jimmy laughed. A lock of shiny, dark hair fell over an eyebrow to lend a rakish appearance to his handsome face. With his good looks and height, he easily could have graced the pages of a fashion magazine. "C'mon, Vanessa, hit harder. You won't be fighting the girls. You have to be able to trade more than a few punches with a man."

That got to her. Was he calling her a sissy? A wimp? Vanessa took pride in her ability to adapt the various fighting styles and techniques Jimmy insisted on teaching and make them her own. Because of her family's wealth and her days spent strutting down the catwalk or preening in front of a camera, most people thought she was eye candy and about as useful as a Christmas tree ornament in the middle of spring. She knew that nothing could be farther from the truth.

With the Gotham Roses and some of her wealthy friends, she raised hundreds of thousands of dollars every year for her favorite charity, The Golden Key Foundation for Battered Women, and several others. The bottom line was that her training, her important charity work and the exciting undercover missions all made her life worthwhile.

Balancing herself, she threw her body into the barrage of punches she aimed at his torso. Jimmy's corresponding grunts as he scrambled to block the blows were music to her ears.

"Good job!" he called out, mixing things up with a few punches of his own. "Next time, don't make me ask for it. If you're in a situation where you have to throw a punch, you need to give it all you've got. You might not get another chance."

At Vanessa's acknowledgement, his hand snaked out to shift her balance and throw her. She flew through the air to land sprawled on her left hip in an ungraceful heap. Because she knew how to fall, she wasn't hurt. As Jimmy advanced, two well-aimed kicks kept him from getting too close. She scrambled to her feet, lifting her arms to block.

"That's enough for today." Jimmy pulled the Velcro on the pads covering his arms and drew them off. "Good work overall, but you're a bit distracted, Vanessa. What's wrong?"

Other than the fact that she'd spent a good part of her morning arguing with her little sister, Michelle, and it had gotten her nowhere, there was the distinct possibility of an upcoming mission. Vanessa met Jimmy's gaze and smiled. "I guess I'm just excited. I'm having tea with Renee. She wants to discuss a new project."

"I see." Jimmy patted her on the shoulder, a knowing look in his eyes. "Whatever it is, I know you'll give it the attention it deserves."

"Of course," she agreed. Pulling apart the Velcro on her own padding, she drew it down and off her arms. Her gaze dropped to her index finger and she cursed under her breath. The nail had broken off at her fingertip. In the heat of their sparring she hadn't noticed.

Jimmy moved close to examine it. "I don't see any blood," he murmured, his dark eyes sparkling. "And those beautiful nails wouldn't look half so good on a corpse."

Glowering at him, Vanessa threw a playful punch

to his wide shoulder. She knew what he was getting at. He'd told her on more than one occasion that her little vanities, which included the highlighted brown hair hanging past her shoulders, her long nails and the four-inch heels she loved, could make it difficult for her to defend herself. Jimmy's comments had only made her work that much harder to hone her skills. She didn't need Jimmy to tell her that she was good at defending herself.

"Just keep your focus on your opponent," he chided gently.

"I will," she promised.

"And good luck on your project."

"Thanks, Jimmy." She leaned forward to plant a little kiss on his cheek. He didn't move, but she sensed him waiting defensively to see if she would try to press herself against him, as had other Gotham Roses who affectionately called him The Heartbreaker.

Jimmy was extremely loyal to his wife, something that many of the wealthy socialites in the Gotham Roses couldn't understand. Vanessa could. Her father, Manfred Dawson III, was still married to her mother, Lonette, and from all appearances, neither had ever been unfaithful. A number of her wealthy friends' parents had been married and divorced so many times that fidelity was almost a novelty.

"Tell Linda I said hello," she murmured, tossing the arm pads into Jimmy's box of athletic aids. She hurried to the dressing room, excitement building within her. She was ready for a challenge.

By the time Vanessa arrived at Renee's private dining room, she'd filed the tip of the broken nail and changed into a pink dress designed by DooRi, an up-and-coming designer friend who had been featured in *Chic* magazine. The dress had a plunging neckline accented with lace, and a drop-waisted skirt with a gathered, asymmetrical hem. She'd twisted her hair into a roll and stepped into her strappy, pink suede Manolo Blahniks to complete her outfit. Slightly distracted, Renee looked fashionably elegant in a fitted, black Sonia Rykiel suit with the trademark knotted bow appliquéd onto the left side of her jacket.

She was already seated at the linen-covered dining table. At the sight of Vanessa, she stood, and they embraced.

"Is everything all right?" Vanessa asked, as Renee commandeered a Verne porcelain teapot with a nautical theme inspired by Jules Verne's *20,000 Leagues Under the Sea.*

Pouring tea, Renee flashed her usual, serenely confident smile. "Things are perfect. Of course we're still trying to catch the Duke, and life is just a little crazy as could be expected with Pres's return. Then there's a minor annoyance or two that I'm *handling*." Her tone deepened and she cut her comment abruptly.

Vanessa knew that Renee and the Governess suspected that the Duke was a wealthy criminal who controlled most of the corruption that went on in moneyed circles. The members of the undercover organization were determined to bring him down, but so far, he'd managed to keep his identity secret.

Observing Renee, Vanessa hoped that the minor annoyances that Renee was referring to had nothing to do with her or the undercover project she sensed just over the horizon. It took a lot to shake Renee Dalton Sinclair and distract her from her work at the Gotham Rose Club. Whether she admitted it or not, something pretty serious was going on.

Since Renee obviously didn't want to talk about it, Vanessa accepted her cup of tea and asked, "Did you get a chance to look at my proposal for a fall charity ball at the Waldorf-Astoria? With all of the Gotham Rose charities to benefit, it would be the event of the season. Then there's the fact that I've personally lined up several friends and family members who would love to attend."

Renee offered Vanessa the tray filled with pastries. "Vanessa, your proposal is an excellent one. Of course it would be good for the Gotham Rose Club. I've already asked Olivia to make some calls and gather preliminary dates. With the number of people our members are capable of drawing to such an event, we're looking at locations that can service a large crowd."

Beaming, Vanessa leaned forward, careful to keep her elbows off the table. "Cool. I can hardly wait to tell the staff over at my foundation. It's been a hard year for them."

"For everyone," Renee corrected.

Vanessa was certain she was talking about more than the various charities the Gotham Rose Club championed and served. Someone had nearly killed Agent Emma Bosworth at a post-Oscar party in L.A. several months ago. The main suspect was the Duke.

"When we've got more information, we'll meet with everyone and make some decisions. Is that satisfactory?"

"Yes. I can see you're on top of this."

"Of course." Renee smiled confidently. "The work we do is very important." They sipped tea in companionable silence. "How's school?" Renee asked a bit too smoothly. "You were working toward a business degree?"

Vanessa explained that if she went full time, she was about a year and a half from getting her business degree at Columbia University. She added that she'd taken the summer off to focus on the charity ball.

Renee threw Vanessa a rueful glance. "As I'm sure you've guessed, there's something else I need to discuss with you." Vanessa nodded and Renee went on. "The Governess has another project and she asked for you personally."

"Really?" Flattered, Vanessa resisted the urge to hunch forward. She was never quite sure how people got picked for the undercover assignments, but she'd had two within the past couple of years.

On her last assignment she'd worked alone, planting bugs and identifying records and files that proved that one former classmate's father's business was illegally dumping chemicals and poisoning the environment. Now she was hoping for something more exciting.

"So tell me about this assignment," Vanessa prompted, anxious to hear the specifics. It wasn't like Renee to hold back on the details.

"As you know, our assignments are important and involve real danger." Renee paused, her blue eyes full of concern. "It's a modeling assignment. If you accept," Renee explained, "it'll take you back to the world you left a couple of years ago. It's even been arranged for you to get a contract to model swimsuits in the coveted *Inside Sports* Swimsuit Fantasy Edition."

Vanessa's chest constricted. She found it hard to swallow past the thickness in her throat. Considering the fact that she hadn't modeled for two years and there were many younger models clamoring for the *Inside Sports* swimsuit edition, the contract was quite an achievement. However, after she'd left the glittering yet caustic world of modeling and spent months recovering in a private clinic, she'd promised herself that she never had to go back. She'd modeled from the time she was fifteen until she was nearly twenty-five, and between the job, the people and life she was exposed to, she'd nearly died at least twice. Others hadn't been so lucky.

Was she really strong enough to go back into that world and stay focused enough to complete a successful undercover mission? She'd never told anyone about everything that had happened to her, everything she'd done, but there had been rumors. Regarding Renee carefully, Vanessa bit the inside of her mouth.

It was more than likely that Renee knew all about her exploits. She might even have pictures. Renee had a number of resources at her fingertips. When she'd asked Vanessa to join the Gotham Rose Club, she'd told her that all the club's members underwent background checks. Vanessa had been admitted, but that didn't mean Renee knew about her struggle with drug addiction.

"Vanessa?" Renee prompted.

Vanessa stood. There was a polite knock and the dining room door swished open as the maid came back with more hot water. Vanessa felt the blood pound in her ears.

Renee extended a hand to briefly cover Vanessa's. "Perhaps you should speak to the Governess's representative and hear the details before you make your decision."

Vanessa nodded. Excusing herself, Renee whispered instructions to the maid. With a nod, the maid refilled the teapot and left the room.

Vanessa forced her body back down into the chair. Lifting her dainty, gold-and-blue accented cup, she took a large sip of the hot liquid, grimacing as it scalded the inside of her mouth.

The dining room door swished open once more. "Excuse me, ladies," a strong male voice projected from the doorway. "Mrs. Sinclair? Ms. Dawson? I'm Cody Mackenzie from the DEA's Miami Field Division and I've been sent by the Governess."

Vanessa set the cup back into the saucer. Her

gaze riveted on the handsome, golden brown man standing in the doorway. The blue, off-the-rack designer suit he wore enhanced his muscular build. Apparently the DEA was attracting better-looking agents these days.

He took in her carefully made up face, the plunging neckline edging her full breasts and the long length of leg revealed by the asymmetrical hemline of her dress. Was that censure in his gaze?

Nodding, Renee regarded him calmly. "Mr. Mackenzie, I'm Renee Dalton Sinclair and this is Vanessa Dawson. Please join us. Tea?" When he declined, she gestured him to a chair. "I wanted Vanessa to meet you and get a rough idea of the mission."

Mackenzie walked to the table to regard Vanessa with dark, combative eyes. "Have you seen the newspapers? Did you read about the two models who were stabbed to death and their apartments ransacked? The DEA thinks that both models were mules in a powerful drug ring."

Pushing her back against the chair until it was ramrod straight, Vanessa answered that she hadn't. She'd become so depressed by the things she read in the news that she avoided it, like an ostrich with its head stuck in the sand. She turned to face Renee, ready to stop Mackenzie from springing the trap she saw closing around her.

"I—I'm not interested, Renee." *I can't go back.*

Mackenzie kept talking. "Both models lived in apartments on Ocean Drive. The first was a new model named Bianca Moore. The second was a veteran model named Gena Chadwick," he said. He pointed his finger at Vanessa. "You knew her. She was a friend of yours."

Vanessa gasped at the names. Her eyes burned. Gena had been her roommate and companion on several assignments when she modeled for Echelon Models.

In her mind's eye, she could see the vivacious Gena with her thick, chestnut-brown hair and her vivid, green eyes. They'd been good friends, but fear of being pulled back into the modeling life had kept Vanessa from maintaining contact with Gena. Had some crazed maniac gotten hold of Gena and Bianca, or had the women been involved in something as dangerous as smuggling drugs? And why? A mixture of grief, anger and outrage burned in her stomach.

Standing, Renee rounded the table to put a comforting hand on Vanessa's shoulder. "There's still time to help the other models being drawn into this and the people who get hooked on the drugs brought into this country," she said. "I hope you can suspend your grief long enough to reconsider. Many lives are at stake."

Renee's words hit Vanessa hard. She had to do something, didn't she? She'd been wild in her modeling days, and had developed a coke addiction between partying and trying to stay thin. Vanessa was ashamed, but knew she wasn't unique with her problem. Many of her wealthy friends and fellow models had abused drugs. At least Vanessa had sought help and recovered.

"I can understand why you might hesitate to put yourself back into such a situation," Renee said carefully, "but you're stronger now and more mature. You've learned a lot through your training here."

Vanessa closed her eyes and considered what was at stake. She risked being drawn back into the drug scene. Investigating the drug ring also involved the personal risk of being killed, like Gena and Bianca. But with the vicious murders of those models and the fact that her little sister Michelle was hell-bent on a modeling career, could she really refuse the assignment?

Chapter 2

Still somewhat shaken that she'd agreed to the assignment, Vanessa sat in the Gotham Rose basement consultation room, trying to concentrate on the mission file Renee had given her. She needed to have her head examined. She was committed to keeping her word, but deep inside she wanted to skip out of the room as fast as her pink suede shoes would take her. The invisible bond of her conscience was the only thing that kept her glued to the chair.

Across the table from her, Cody Mackenzie's mere presence crowded the room. A cloud of negative vibes hovered over his head and threatened to drench everyone in the room. When he glanced her way, there was an unpleasant expression on his face. His nostrils flared and the corner of his wide mouth curled. He looked like he'd been sucking lemons. What was his problem?

Vanessa thought back on everything that had happened since Mackenzie appeared. Yes, she'd initially refused the assignment, but that was her right and she'd had good reasons. Yes, she'd weathered some emotional moments when she'd heard about poor Gena and her friend, but she'd done nothing to earn Mackenzie's enmity.

On a large media screen at the front of the room, Renee projected pictures and provided details. Vanessa stared at the pictures of the models: both had been beaten, raped and stabbed to death. There'd been no mercy or dignity in what they had endured before death set them free.

Her eyelids stung. Balling her fists, she parted her lips and forced air into her lungs.

The next group of pictures centered on the upscale building on Ocean Drive in Miami where the models had had apartments. With the Novak sofa and chair and the Milan coffee tables in the living room, Gena's apartment was a study in soothing blues and hardwood floors. Vanessa was certain that it had been designed and decorated by a professional.

One or more of a very different kind of professional had destroyed Gena's apartment, too. The sofa and all the chairs in the place had been cut with a knife and viciously ripped to shreds. Someone had even taken the seats and backs off the chairs and ripped the carpet with razors. The kitchen was a mess of broken glass and china. Silverware littered the floor. Nothing in the apartment remained intact.

"They certainly found what they were looking for," Mackenzie said roughly, breaking the stark silence.

Renee flicked her remote ahead to a picture of a clear glass container that had been glued together. The label on the front read Caribbean Mama Spice Mix.

"I imagine that this jar never held the kind of spice that goes on food," Renee remarked dryly. "The lab analyzed the pieces of glass that formed this container and found they were coated with cocaine. It seems likely that the girls transported the cocaine into the country in spice jars like this. It's probably not the only type of product container used. Judging by the way their apartments and belongings were searched and destroyed, the Miami Field Division, MFD, thinks the girls may have messed up the delivery somehow and gotten themselves killed. The girls had just returned from a trip to the Bahamas. They cruised regularly on yachts owned by people high up in the fashion and music industries. MFD's not sure which boat they were on, because all their friends and associates have suddenly developed acute cases of amnesia."

Vanessa's throat tightened. If she'd stayed in modeling and continued everything she'd been doing, she could have been one of the victims. "So who are we after?"

As Renee clicked a new picture onto the screen, Cody spoke. "We're after a ring headed or financed by someone in the upper echelons of society or highly placed in Miami business or in the music industry. We have more than one suspect." He pointed to the picture on the screen. "This is Hector Guerra. He came up from the streets of Miami with a past that includes the Street Killers and 114th Avenue Boys. His club and hip-hop clothing lines have made him popular. The models attended several of his parties. His clothing lines could provide an excellent cover for transporting drugs."

Vanessa studied the photo of the tall, lean, Latino man. Hooded brows and beautifully shaped lips dominated his golden-skinned face. He was one of the designers her sister, Michelle, adored and the type of man that would have attracted Gena.

Taye Rollins, also known as Hot T, was the man

in the next photo. Renee explained that the hip-hop artist, record producer and clothing designer had come up from the Street Killers gang of Miami, and now employed former gang members, and sponsored and produced artists coming out of Miami street gangs. He'd also been spotted at several events with an entourage that included both of the models.

Vanessa owned several of Taye's CDs. His compositions were edgy, sexy and innovative. With skin the color of warm milk chocolate, he was attractive and had a smile that pulled at something deep inside her. Could the man be that provocative in person? She doubted it.

In the next photo, Caulfield Carouthers was blond with piercing, gray eyes. Vanessa knew the publishing heir through his snobby sister, Lindy, who'd gone to high school with her. According to the file, his lifestyle and gambling habit had negatively affected his publishing empire. He hung out with people in the fast lane and had been seen with several of the other suspects. He'd also had an affair with Bianca a couple of years ago.

Vanessa was surprised when a photo of dark-haired, heavyset, pugnacious-faced movie producer Benton Lansing appeared on the screen. According to Mackenzie, Benton hung out and partied with Taye and the other suspects. His last two movies had flopped and he was trying to get funding for another. He could be trying to finance his next picture with drug money.

Last, but not least, was Garrett Sutter, the Sutter Distillery heir. Vanessa had met him and been present at a few society functions he'd also attended. He mostly kept to himself. Being in the wrong place at the wrong time with the wrong people had landed him on the DEA's suspect list.

"So exactly what is my assignment?" Vanessa asked.

Renee placed the remote on the table. Calm and confident, she faced them directly. An inner fire lit her royal-blue eyes. "You're to go to Miami with Agent Mackenzie. There, you will move into the condo complex on Ocean Drive and get to know the models on the party circuit. Find out what you can about Gena and Bianca's activities. Your goal is to get a lead on this drug operation, work with Cody to identify its members, and get the evidence we need. Mackenzie will help photograph you and several other models for the swimsuit edition of *Inside Sports*."

For the first time, Vanessa felt excited at the chance to grace the cover of *Inside Sports*. The assignment stoked her competitive streak. Her gaze darted to Renee. That the Governess and her contacts had managed such a coup was quite a bonus. The modeling career she'd tanked was returning with a bang.

"Agent Mackenzie, Vanessa, I know that you two have just met, but you were each considered the best we could find for this assignment. Mackenzie, your work with the DEA in Miami has been highly commended. You must also be proud to have placed your photos in various art and photography magazines."

Mackenzie closed his briefing file. "Thank you. But now we've got a job to do."

"I'd already planned to take two independent study classes in the upcoming term at school, but I'll need at least a day to square things with my family," Vanessa put in quickly, making a concerted effort to avoid the agent's gaze. Still, she felt the weight of it and suppressed the impulse to explain. She didn't owe him an explanation.

"A day or two is fine," Renee informed them. "Vanessa, you'll need to at least check in with Erin Branch at the MFD. Both your *Inside Sports* contract and the details on where you'll be staying can be found in your file. Any questions?"

Mackenzie asked about the chain of command on and off the team.

Matter-of-factly Renee faced him. "This is a joint

operation between the Gotham Roses and the DEA. You're considered equals. Mackenzie's supervisor at the MFD and I expect to be kept up to date on your progress. The MFD is available to provide you with any local help and backup you might need. Mackenzie, you're still expected to follow DEA rules and procedures. We've already cleared your use of our technology and wardrobe for this assignment with your supervisor. Vanessa, you know our rules of operation. You'll turn over your evidence to the MFD. Otherwise, you're on your own."

Renee's statements didn't surprise Vanessa. She'd worked alone on the last assignment. All of the women in the club's undercover organization were trained and capable of working alone. The wild card here was Cody Mackenzie. Would he make the assignment a breeze, or become a full-blown pain in the ass?

"If there's nothing further, Alan's got a few gadgets for you and Kristi's worked up a wardrobe profile and several additions for both of you." Standing, Renee shook their hands. "Good luck."

Down the hall from the consultation room, Alan Burke was waiting for them in his lab. His eyes sparkled as he showed Vanessa a set of press-on nails decorated with an intricate swirling crystal design.

Thinking about the nail she'd broken while sparring with Jimmy, she suppressed a smile. Alan was good at customizing his gadgets to fit his customer's personalities and lifestyles. When Alan showed her that parts of the detailed design on the nails were actually electronic bugs that could be peeled off and stuck on various surfaces, she nodded approvingly.

Vanessa also received a slim gold-colored cell phone that functioned as a Global Positioning System device, a speaker and recorder for the bugs from the fingernails, and a gadget for opening electronic locks and accessing computer systems. *Cool.*

Alan opened a slim jewelry box and drew out a fourteen-carat gold watch with a detailed antique rose design on the face. "Press the side button in firmly three times in succession, and Agent Mackenzie and your backup team will know that you need help. It's your panic button. It sends out a homing signal, too, if you only press it twice."

"I like it." Vanessa fitted the delicate watch onto her wrist and snapped the clasp closed. "Thanks, Alan. For everything."

Alan drew another box from his workbench and gave it to Mackenzie. "Your watch. It does everything Vanessa's watch does." The watch was a Movado. As Mackenzie put it on, Alan drew another package from the alcove on his desk. Mackenzie opened the next package to reveal a 35mm camera. He eyed Alan cautiously. "A camera?"

"A camera that enables you to see in any light. It's got built-in night vision and a few extra buttons." Alan showed him a row of small buttons on the back of the camera. "Hit number one and your subject gets a knockout mist. Make sure you're within two feet. Hit number two, and it shoots a paralyzing dart."

"And number three?" Mackenzie asked, his finger close to the button.

Alan's expression held a dare. "Press that and count to three, throw the camera as hard as you can, and run like hell!"

"A grenade?" Mackenzie's fingers moved far away from the row of buttons.

Alan grinned. "For all intents and purposes."

Mackenzie stepped forward to carefully place the camera back on Alan's workbench. "This thing is some piece of work."

Alan lifted the camera from the table, handling it carelessly. Mackenzie and Vanessa shot him incredulous looks. "The camera is quite safe to use," Alan informed them. "There's a safety switch along the side here," he said, fingered a sliding bar. "None of the extra features work until you take the safety off."

Vanessa released a sigh of relief. "Do you have any other gadgets for Agent Mackenzie?"

Alan glanced back at Mackenzie. "Not at the moment, but I'd love the chance to whip something up just for *him*."

Vanessa stared. Had Alan just made a pass at Mackenzie? Hostile elements colored Mackenzie's expression as he met Alan's gaze.

Damn, tough break for Alan. Vanessa had instinctively known that Mackenzie was straight. She cleared her throat. "Thanks again, Alan. We'd better see what Kristi's got for us."

Mackenzie thanked Alan. Then he and Vanessa made their exit. Outside the room, Mackenzie rolled his shoulders and said just under his breath, "Your Alan's got a little sugar in his tank."

Vanessa hated all the euphemisms used to describe men like Alan. Her gaze hardened. "If you mean he's gay, yes, but he's never tried to force it on anyone."

"And how would you know?"

"We don't just work together. Alan is a friend," she said, steel creeping into her tone.

Acknowledging her statement with a nod of his head, Mackenzie fell quiet as they made their way to Kristi's office.

Vanessa introduced the agent to Kristi—adding

that she was Alan's sister, in case Mackenzie planned to make any more comments about him—and they sat down.

Kristi opened a leather file and drew out a list and a set of color pictures. "For this assignment I selected items that go with the clothes you have, but I tried to pump you up a little more," she told Vanessa. "You already have fabulous instincts when it comes to fashion. This time, you want to make more of a statement and get the right kind of attention."

Vanessa liked clothes. It was one of the things that had made her enjoy modeling. She looked at the first designer outfit. It was a slinky, sexy white DooRi wrap dress. Vanessa flipped through the rest of the file, her smile growing. Kristi had included items from a number of her favorite designers, including bustier dresses and silk camisoles from Dolce & Gabbana, classic but sexy gowns from Versace, Vera Wang, Valentino couture, Prada, Manolo Blahnik, and Jimmy Choo. Just about ready to swoon with satisfaction, she turned to Kristi.

"Thanks, I love this wardrobe!"

"I thought you would." Kristi beamed back at her, something just short of envy in her eyes. She loved clothes just as much as Vanessa did. Sometimes the two of them went to fashion shows together.

Drawing another folder from the leather file,

Kristi handed it to Mackenzie. "Agent Mackenzie, as the photographer on this project, your wardrobe makes much less of a statement. I've been told that you prefer casual wear. Therefore, I've put together a wardrobe centered on relaxed easy wear by Sean John and Fubu. For dress, I added a couple of Ralph Lauren suits, and a tuxedo from his Mister shop. For shoes, Nike Air Force Ones, Johnston & Murphy slip-ons, and Prada dress shoes. What do you think?"

"Fine by me."

"I like the colors you chose for Agent Mackenzie," Vanessa added. "They highlight his skin tone."

Mackenzie looked at Vanessa with thinly veiled surprise, or perhaps annoyance. She had a feeling he didn't appreciate her input on his wardrobe. She met his gaze squarely, intuitively aware that working with him meant she'd have to earn his respect and fight for equal footing.

But first, she'd have to loosen him up.

Chapter 3

Tired from a late night out with her friends, Vanessa dragged herself out of bed at eleven the next morning and began to pack the clothes Kristi had sent over. The rest would be shipped to her new apartment in Miami.

After giving her word to Renee and signing the magazine contract, Vanessa was prepared to go through with the assignment, no matter what. As she showered and got ready for an early dinner at her parents' home, she rehearsed how she would tell her father that she was going back into modeling. She was an adult, already twenty-seven, and her career choice shouldn't be his business, but she knew he wouldn't be happy.

Manfred Dawson tried to run his family the way he ran his successful real estate business, with mixed success. Her mother was good at appearing to toe the line while managing to get exceptions for the things she really wanted to do. Michelle, Vanessa's fourteen-year-old sister, was Daddy's girl. She generally got what she wanted, but she could forget getting anything that might grant her a measure of independence.

Vanessa was the rebel in the family. She'd gone head to head with her father about her modeling career and had proceeded against his wishes at the age of fifteen. He'd considered having his daughter in the modeling business tantamount to her selling her body for money. When the barely eighteen-year-old Vanessa's affair with the head of Savoy Models was exposed, she was cut out of her family allowance for her refusal to quit the business as her father demanded. She thanked God that her father knew nothing about her cocaine addiction and recovery in the private clinic in upstate New York.

As Vanessa expertly applied foundation and blush, she gave up on finding any magic words to break it gently to her father. The best option lay in finding the right moment, dropping the bomb and going for damage control if he did explode. Coating her lips with Raspberry Ice gloss, she blotted them and spread her mouth into a smile. What was the worst he could do, anyway?

Using the remote to send the clothes in her closet whizzing by for her inspection, she answered her own question. Her father would use the big threat he always used. He'd threaten to cut her off from the family fortune. His threat and her determination to be independent had prompted her to enroll in Columbia University and work fulltime toward a business degree.

Going to college had given her that much more confidence in her ability to take care of herself and eventually it had gotten her back into her family's good graces. After going year round and taking extra classes, she had only a year and a half more before getting a bachelor's degree in business administration. The only problem was that she had no idea what kind of business she wanted to be in.

After halting the parade of clothes and selecting a silk, ruby-colored Versace camisole and a soft, flowered silk Cavalli wrap skirt, she stepped into the shoes closet on her left and found a matching red pair of Manolos.

Crossing the room, she caught sight of herself in the mirror. She usually liked more meat on her five-foot-eleven-inch frame, but she was just about the right size for the cameras. Maybe catching a bug on that family cruise to the Mediterranean last month hadn't been such a bad thing after all. Now all she had to do was watch what she ate.

By the time she'd dressed and styled her sandy brown, golden-streaked hair and attended to some charity matters in her home office, her father's chauffer was waiting in the car downstairs. Stuffing her lipstick and keys into her Gucci Hobo bag, she hurried downstairs to the car.

At her parents' home in an exclusive section of Scarsdale, Vanessa greeted Robert, the butler, and made her way in. Her parents were relaxing and getting ready for dinner in the large living area they used to entertain guests.

"You look wonderful," her mother said, moving from her place on the sofa in front of the floor-to-ceiling windows to hug and kiss Vanessa.

In a classic, pink Chanel suit, Lonette Dawson was gorgeous. The highlights in her sandy brown hair were subtler than Vanessa's, her eyes were sienna brown instead of hazel and her figure was more rounded, but they looked like sisters.

"You look beautiful, too, Mama," Vanessa murmured, returning the kiss on the cheek. She approached her dad, who was leaning back on the sofa in a navy, checked Perry Ellis suit. The financial and real estate sections of the paper were close to his fingers, but he was making an effort to give the family all of his attention.

"Daddy, how are you?" she said, kissing his cheek.

"I'll be better when this deal I'm working on goes through," he noted irritably. He paused and a charming, apologetic smile transformed his face. "Sorry, sweetheart, that has nothing to do with you. How's school?"

"You know I took the summer off to concentrate on my charity work with the Gotham Rose Club."

"Vanessa will have her degree in another year and a half," her mother said, taking Vanessa's hand and urging her to a spot on the couch. "Want something to drink?"

Vanessa wet her lips. Tonight she needed all her faculties. "Ginger ale?" At the bar, Robert was already filling a glass for her.

Her father's hazel eyes regarded her thoughtfully. "So what will you do when you get this degree from Columbia? You want a job with the company?"

Vanessa felt the walls closing in. Working for the family business would put her right under her father's thumb. "No—at least not right now. I was thinking that I could manage my portfolio."

"There's not much in it, is there? Nothing except for the stock you've gotten for Christmases and birthdays," he remarked. "You don't get control of the trust fund until you're thirty and I'm pretty sure you haven't saved any of your family allowance."

"There's the money my mother left her," her mother put in quickly.

"That wasn't enough to cover Vanessa's clothing allowance for more than a few years," her father countered.

Normally, it would be true, but Vanessa had plans for independence that went a long way towards helping her pass up on that extra pair of designer shoes or the latest bag. "Actually, I used some of the family allowance toward the Gotham Roses and for schooling and living expenses." Using the condo she'd inherited from her grandmother as her home, she'd tied the inherited funds into investments that she used to pay the taxes. Accepting the ginger ale from Robert and thanking him, she spoke up for herself.

Newfound respect crept into her father's eyes. "Good. I parlayed less into enough of a fortune to win the business over your Uncle Marvin."

Having heard the particular story of how he made his wealth more times than she cared to count, Vanessa held her breath. Her mother rolled her eyes.

Relief came from an unlikely source. Dressed in a pink tank and crinkled silk miniskirt, Michelle burst into the room, interrupting her father's lecture. A couple of pages of the newspaper dangled from Michelle's fingers and her gaze skewered Vanessa.

"Michelle, how many times have I told you, it's not ladylike to run about the house?" Lonette Dawson's voice carried an edge.

"Sorry, Mama. I'll try to remember next time. I was just so excited about what I read in the Rubi Cho *In the Know* column in today's *New York Reporter.* She says that the ink on the contract is almost dry and the most memorable sweetheart from the Sweetheart Dreams Catalog is coming back to star in the *Inside Sports* swimsuit edition." With a hand on one hip, Michelle turned accusing eyes on Vanessa. "That's you, isn't it, Vanessa? Are you going to be in the *Inside Sports* swimsuit edition?"

Vanessa had signed the contract only yesterday. How had Rubi Cho gotten wind of it so quickly? For the second time that evening, her voice stuck in her throat. "I—I—" She cleared her throat. There was nothing to do but own up to it. "Yes. I was going to announce it after dinner," she admitted, facing her family with her head up and her shoulders squared. "Keifer Jonas, the photographer who did several of my most famous shots, asked me personally," she lied. "They're paying a lot of money that I can put in my portfolio and it's a really good opportunity. I'll be back before next semester starts. Mom, Dad, I—I just couldn't pass it up."

Brows drawing together like thunderclouds, her father's eyes sparked with anger. "Vanessa, I thought that phase of your life was over. The last thing this family needs is our version of Paris Hilton in the limelight. It's time to think of starting a family or helping expand the family business. Aren't you getting a little old for modeling?"

Vanessa winced, his words burning her like acid.

"Mannie…" Lonette's soft voice halted her husband's tirade. She moved over to Vanessa on the couch and took her hand. "We're concerned about you, Vanessa. We certainly have enough money that you don't have to work. You know that, and your father doesn't ask that much in return. Are you sure you want to do this?"

"Yes, and I'm not planning to do anything to make headlines or embarrass the family," Vanessa answered, her voice confident.

"I'm still remembering ninety-five percent of your body on display in a popular magazine, and the gossip headlines when you were a minor, having an affair with the head of that modeling agency. And what about the wild parties and the boyfriend-turned-stalker? I can't see *you* doing anything without attracting headlines," her father said, snapping his fingers and reaching for the paper still dangling from Michelle's hand.

Vanessa cringed. Who but her father could dismiss her life with such negativity?

"What about me?" Michelle asked, giving her father the paper. "I want to go into modeling, too. People my age model all the time. I could go down on location with Vanessa and make some contacts—"

"Michelle, we've already had this discussion," Lonette said, regarding her daughter sternly. "That's not the sort of life we want for you."

Steeped in déjà vu, Vanessa knew how Michelle felt. The life her parents demanded was comparable to a padded cell.

Right now though, with her current assignment and what she knew about the modeling world, she was glad her parents were keeping Michelle out of it. She couldn't stand the thought of Michelle going through all that she had.

"You guys never let me do anything!" Michelle whined. Tears filled her eyes. "When Vanessa started—"

Manfred Dawson's heavy voice cut through her objections. "Michelle, the answer is *no*. Don't ask again."

Just then, Robert appeared in the doorway to announce dinner, and as the family headed for the dining room, a pouting Michelle ran off to her room.

Vanessa sat through a strained, awkward dinner
with her parents. Her appetite gone, she pushed
grilled salmon with creamed dill sauce, stir-fried
green beans and a twice-baked potato around on
her plate.

Her father frowned every time he looked at her.
It was a silent reproach. Nothing she said reached
him. She found herself wondering, when had he
ever smiled at her and been supportive? Only when
she did as he dictated. He wanted a puppet, not a
daughter.

Her mother chattered on about things—the next
ball, the garden club meeting and her church work.
When her gaze met Vanessa's there was a sort of
desperation in her eyes. Lonette really hated discord
among her family. After an initial effort to resolve
things, her usual solution was to try to act as if nothing had happened and hope it would go away. It
never worked.

Vanessa refused the crème brûlée dessert and got
ready to leave. She loved her parents, but she had a
job to do. A job she couldn't tell them about.

Before she left, Vanessa stopped by Michelle's
room to talk and try to smooth things over. At first,

Michelle was too angry to say much, but when she heard that Vanessa was leaving for Miami in the morning, she turned red-rimmed eyes on her sister and said, "I thought you said that you'd never go back, that it was full of nothing but bad memories?"

Vanessa nodded. "I did, and I meant it, but I have something important to do. I'm not just going back to model, I'm going back to do something for a friend and I gave my word."

"What are you going to do?" Michelle asked, curiosity in her eyes as she searched Vanessa's face. "You can tell me."

Vanessa knew better than to play this game. "No, I can't. Just take my word for it."

Michelle's eyes sparkled with tears. "You're going to leave me here with them. Let me come with you! I won't be any trouble. I know how to take care of myself."

Nothing was further from the truth. Smoothing her sister's hair, Vanessa leaned in and hugged her. "I can't. They'd disown me if I did that."

"They wouldn't do that," Michelle said. "Daddy keeps taking away the money and you still keep doing what you want."

Vanessa met her sister's gaze. "You're right," she admitted. "I do keep doing what I have to do. I'm an adult. Daddy thinks he knows what's best for me, but he's lived his life and made his own decisions. Do you see? I've got to do what I think is best, even if it's a mistake."

Michelle's next question haunted Vanessa all the way back to her condo. "Is this modeling job a mistake?"

Vanessa left New York on a morning flight to Miami. There, she picked up the red Jag convertible they'd leased for her. Afterward, she followed the leasing agent's directions to her new condo on Ocean Drive.

As the concierge unloaded her luggage and the valet accepted her keys, Vanessa studied the building where the models had been killed. The large, three-story structure was big enough to guarantee some privacy, but nothing like the high-rises that dotted Ocean Drive. Part of the building was set in a lush, tropical garden, the rest on the beach.

A blue-uniformed man opened the lobby door and Vanessa stepped into the building wearing Seven for All Mankind custom jeans made to fit her curvy butt just right and a lilac silk tank top. Her heels clicked as she crossed a marbled lobby to stop at the service desk and get directions to her condo. Minutes later, she was back outside in the hot sun, rounding the building to stop in front of her unit.

A tall blonde in dark glasses, swim shorts and a bikini top came out of the next unit and pulled the door shut. "Moving in?" she asked, smiling.

Recognizing one of the models to be photographed for *Inside Sports*, Vanessa returned the smile. "Yes. I'm Vanessa. How are you?"

"Right now, I'm just getting started on the fun." The blonde pushed the sunglasses down her nose to peer at Vanessa. "Your hazel eyes…I thought I recognized you. You're Vanessa Dawson, aren't you?"

Flattered, Vanessa felt her smile widen. "Yes, I am."

"I'm Annika LaVatia, fellow model on the *Inside Sports* project." She moved closer. "Welcome to Miami! You'll love this place. It's got everything a girl could want."

"Really?" Vanessa let the question hang in the air, wondering if "everything" included drugs.

"Oh yeah," Annika bubbled on, "I love having my own town house and still being able to get room service, and the waiters bringing the food are hot. Add that you're just steps from the beach, and you can't beat the security. Then there's a bunch of restaurants close by."

"It sounds like a dream." Vanessa fitted her key into the lock. "There's only one thing that could turn this into a nightmare…"

"I can't imagine a thing," Annika said, flipping back a long strand of hair.

"Well, I heard about some models getting killed in a condo on Ocean Drive," Vanessa said cautiously. "A friend of mine insists that this is the place."

"Oh." Annika's voice dropped a few octaves. "This *is* the place," she reluctantly admitted.

"But not the same *unit?*" Vanessa let a note of fear creep into her voice.

"Lord, no. That unit was ripped apart. Besides, it's closer to the beach and it has to be redecorated." Annika looked uncomfortable. "Look, Vanessa, I'm not worried about the same thing happening to me. It's not as if we've got a serial killer hanging out here, waiting to murder models. Those girls were wild and into some heavy stuff. They knew some bad people, too. Maybe they just pissed off the wrong guys."

"Maybe." Vanessa's jaw snapped shut. It was hard not to give in to the righteous anger growing inside of her and tell Annika that no one deserved to die the way Gena and Bianca had.

"Well, it was nice meeting you, Vanessa." Annika was obviously through with the subject. She pushed her sunglasses back up on her nose. "I guess I'll see you around."

Annika strolled off toward the beach, leaving Vanessa wondering if she should have pushed for more information.

Unlocking the door, she stepped onto the oak hardwood floor of an entryway that opened onto an expansive room with floor-to-ceiling windows showcasing a sun-filled view of the beach. Tearing her gaze away, she took in modular white chairs and a white Novak sofa, with oak accents dotting the room. The Chablis table set blended in to create vivid and bold lines. She loved this condo already and was looking forward to seeing the rest of it.

The sparkle of sun off the blue water drew Vanessa's gaze. It reminded her of her family's estate on a private beach in Jamaica. She saw Annika stroll up to a woman sunning herself in a yellow string bikini and lean down to talk. The other woman sat up. Then both women turned to look in Vanessa's direction. A chill ran through her as she stepped away from the window. Had she already given herself away?

Chapter 4

Vanessa gave the French Double Slipper Tub in the master bath a longing glance as she used the china-bowl sink on top of the fancy wrought-iron stand. The inviting tub was built for two, but she saw herself relaxing in it alone with a glass of wine and scented candles.

Her face clean, she applied a fresh layer of natural-looking makeup and worked with her hair until it fell past her shoulders in artful disarray. Rummaging through her luggage, she found a white pair of slacks and a light, cotton camisole made of ragged, woven strips of colored fabric. The single gold button on the front hit just below her breasts and left a tantalizing strip of her skin bare. She spritzed it with a dash of cologne. As Vanessa stepped into a pair of Jimmy Choo print slides she added a small Jimmy Choo hobo bag.

Outside, it had grown hotter. In the interest of saving time, Vanessa took a taxi to the trendy Nemo restaurant, with its interactive food bar, dining room and other areas, including the terrace, garden and courtyard. She took a seat at the table that had been reserved in the Loggia, an environmentally controlled area that opened to the garden.

The place was filled with wrought-iron furnishings and modern hanging lamps. All around her, Miami's beautiful denizens chatted, people watched and presumably closed deals. The menu featured several eclectic items with Asian influence. Vanessa decided on wok-charred salmon with roasted pumpkin seeds. Then she ordered a glass of chardonnay and settled in to wait for Mackenzie.

She finally spotted him striding through the entrance of the restaurant in flax-colored slacks and a short-sleeved designer print shirt. The expensive-looking digital camera he'd gotten from Alan dangled from a strap on his shoulder. Several women turned to check him out. Vanessa waved to show him where she was seated. Nodding, he approached the table.

"Sorry if I'm a little late," he murmured as he took his seat. "I stopped by the office to take care of a few things."

"Actually you're right on time," she answered, noting the way he gave her the once-over. She felt like asking, *Do I pass?* At least that sour look was gone from his face.

His gaze lingered on the skin left bare by her top and then fast-forwarded to her face with what seemed a determination to be businesslike. "Did you order?"

She tapped her menu with a raspberry-colored nail. "I waited for you."

"Didn't see anything you liked? If you'd like to go somewhere more exclusive..."

"This place is fine," she answered in surprise. "And it's full of models, tourists and businesspeople. Is the food bad?"

"The food is great." The sour look returned to his face. "I just thought the place might not be up to your usual standards."

"You think I'm a snob." She'd spoken without thinking first, but it explained the sour expression, the curling lip in New York.

"Aren't you?" He kept his tone even, but the look in his eyes made it clear that he didn't like her.

"No, I'm not." Vanessa gritted her teeth. "You

don't know me, Agent Mackenzie, so stop trying to make assumptions. My background might be different from yours, but I've been trained. I know what I'm doing and I'm good at it. If it's too difficult for you to be pleasant on a personal level, try to be professional about us working together."

Annoyance darkened his eyes as he leaned forward over the table. "The last thing I need to do my job is a bored modeling heiress trying to amuse herself by playing secret-agent games."

Vanessa parried that comment with a smile. Mackenzie definitely had his briefs in a bunch. This was not an assignment she'd wanted and he knew it. "Apparently our bosses don't agree. Besides, you know that I had to be convinced to even take this on."

"True—" He was interrupted by the waitress, who had suddenly appeared at their table.

As the waitress bustled off to fill their order, Vanessa asked, "Do you know why I do what I do, Mackenzie? It's not about being rich when so many people are poor. It's about good and evil. Evil is kicking the shit out of good people, and if we don't take a stand and get out and do something about it, no one's going to be able to live on this earth."

He pinned her with his gaze, righteousness simmering in the depths of his brown eyes. "You haven't seen evil. Not in the world you come from. I wasn't raised in the projects or the streets, but we were very poor. My parents scraped and worked hard for everything they got. The strong preyed on the weak. All around me people tried to escape the misery with drugs, booze and gangs. I do what I do because I understand, and I know I can make a difference."

"And you don't think we have the same goals?" Vanessa asked, suddenly aware of the urgency that had crept into her voice. There was no getting through to this man. Her jaw was so tight she could feel a vibration in her teeth.

Mackenzie expelled a noisy breath but didn't answer. When his glance swept over her clothes and exposed skin once more, her hands formed fists.

"So what is your plan for this assignment?" Vanessa asked. She wasn't going to let him distract her from her goal.

Mackenzie shrugged. "Until we get some leads, it's pretty much talking to people and getting next to them."

She wasn't stupid. "Yes, but first we need to know who Gena and Bianca's friends were and who they were hanging out with." Listening to Mackenzie, Vanessa wished she were working this mission alone.

"You're stating the obvious," he said frankly.

Vanessa rolled her eyes and counted to ten. If she had to argue with him about every little thing, what good was he?

Their drinks came and Mackenzie took a long swallow out of his.

"I met Annika LeVatia, one of the other models on the shoot, as I was moving in," she said, trying another tack. "When I told her I was concerned about being in the same building where the models had been killed, she tried to shift the blame to Gena and Bianca because they were wild, knew some bad people and had probably pissed somebody off."

"And?" Mackenzie put his glass back on the table.

"And I got a weird vibe from her. I think she knows more. My credentials may be different from yours, Mackenzie, but I've got very good instincts when it comes to people." *That's how I already know you're a narrow-minded ass.*

He perked up, drew a little notebook and ink pen from his pocket and made a few notes. "Annika has been staying there for about a year. There's a good chance she does know something we could use. I'll keep an eye on her, too." His gaze turned inward. "Let me know if you come up with anything."

Not trusting herself to say more, she sipped her

chardonnay, certain she should have ordered something stronger.

Mackenzie flipped to the front of his notebook. "While I was in the office I put in some time researching and correlating the airplane trips that Gena and Bianca have taken in the past three or four months. There's a steady pattern of visits to the Bahamas, Jamaica and the Virgin Islands. I've already contacted their charge card companies and ordered copies of their charges for that period."

"Good," she commented. "Let me know if you come up with anything."

His head came up and their gazes locked combatively. Neither looked away until the waitress arrived with their food. It was delicious. Fortunately, Vanessa had sense enough to eat only half. The other half she had the waitress pack to go.

She watched Mackenzie eat double-chocolate cheesecake while she nibbled at fresh fruit compote. Her stomach whined. Embarrassed, she hoped he would ignore it.

Mackenzie glanced up, licking the chocolate off his full bottom lip. "Still hungry?"

She set her back against her chair, trying to convince herself that there was nothing erotic about what he was doing. "I have to watch what I eat."

"There's plenty here if you'd like to taste some of this," he offered.

Sizing him up, she wondered whether he was really trying to be nice, or trying to make her feel bad about having to starve herself to stay thin for the camera. "Thanks, but no thanks," she managed to say. She couldn't eat any of it. Being hungry all the time was one of the things she'd hated about being a model.

Vanessa drank all her water and signaled the waitress for more. It helped fill some of the empty space in her stomach.

"When do we start shooting the swimsuit fantasies?" she asked.

"Day after tomorrow, so get some sleep."

Inside, Vanessa bristled. Was he trying to say she looked tired?

"The shooting schedule should be in your welcome packet at the condo," he added.

"Are you doing all of my shots?" she asked, wondering how good he was. Having been away from the industry for more than two years, she hadn't heard of Mackenzie. Her friend Keifer Jonas, the senior photographer on the magazine project, had an excellent reputation and a portfolio to die for.

Mackenzie's glance swept over her once more. This time it was purely professional. "I've got about a third of your beach and studio time. Keifer has the rest."

"Any ideas?" She had to ask. Now that she'd come back to modeling, a lot of her future depended on the success of this magazine shoot.

"There are a couple of suits that specific designers sent down just for you. That'll determine a lot about the setting, hair and makeup."

Checking the food bill, she reached inside her bag for money.

"I make enough to pay for lunch," Mackenzie snapped, reaching for the bill.

"This wasn't a *date*. It was a business meeting," she reminded him. "Loosen up, Mackenzie." She put a fifty in the leather wallet with the bill to cover her food and glass of wine.

He dug a hundred and a twenty out of his pocket. Opening the leather wallet, he drew her fifty out and placed it on the table.

"Oh, grow up!" Vanessa pushed her chair away from the table and stood. With a clicking of her heels, she headed for the exit.

Outside, Mackenzie caught up with her. "Wait, Vanessa," he said. "Look, somehow you bring out the worst in me."

"I could say the same," she shot back. In her heels, she was nearly as tall as he was. Facing him, she could feel the tension simmering between them.

"Let me drop you off," he said, dangling a set of keys. "It'll take a while to get a taxi."

She wanted to say no. She'd had enough of Mackenzie, but common sense prevailed.

When he drove out of the parking lot in a metallic red BMW Z4 convertible, she was glad she'd relented. He didn't complain when she asked him to put the top up to preserve her hairstyle, but a question still occupied her mind. Would she be able to work with him, or would she have to work around him?

Cody was nearly finished with his work in the photography studio when he got the call from Annika. There was a get-together at her complex this evening and she wanted him to come spend time with her, unwind and meet her friends. He seized the opportunity to mingle and check out the condo crowd. He wondered why Vanessa hadn't told him about the party, but since they were still wrestling with being partners, he let it go.

At seven o'clock that evening, Cody entered Ocean Air, the complex's restaurant. The buzz of conversation filled the place. It had been decorated to resemble a deck on a cruise ship with oak paneling everywhere and large, port-hole-shaped windows offering breathtaking views of the ocean. Several people sat on lounge furniture and captains' chairs off to one side of the restaurant and bar. The rest stood in convenient spots and talked while holding drinks.

Cody waded into the crowd of residents that included corporate executives, lawyers, a couple of B-list movie stars and several models. He was glad he'd worn the more expensive Sean John outfit. The dress was mostly business casual, but it was the high-quality designer stuff.

He scanned the faces for people they'd discussed at the briefing and saw none. He didn't see Vanessa, either. Annika was deep in conversation with two women on the far side of the room. As he started toward her, one of the models latched on to his arm and started chattering in his ear about the magazine shoot.

Annika spotted him and came to meet him. Her effusive hug and the quick hello kiss that followed were enough to send the other model on her way.

She didn't know him that well, but Cody took it all in stride. He knew that Annika had been pushing for input on which of her photos would be used in the magazine. So far, she'd been unsuccessful, but she was a determined lady. She was beautiful, with long legs, enhanced breasts and green eyes, but Cody was unaffected. Working with some of the world's most beautiful women on the magazine shoot had made him more discerning in what he wanted in a woman. Annika had a hard edge beneath her beauty that prompted him to examine everything she said and did.

Annika drew him over to the other side of the room and introduced him to her friends Sharon, Tasha and Toni. Toni, an exotic dancer, was the only one who wasn't a model. She had a lush, sexy body that was centerfold material. Cody avoided staring.

The conversation started with the modeling business and moved on to music. Annika made sure that some part of her touched him at all times, and when she started talking about a "smaller gathering" in her condo, he knew what was up.

Cody had been seated for a good half hour before he saw Vanessa. The crystals on her pants sparkled in the light as she stood and talked to a Latino guy. As if she felt his gaze, she looked across the room and saw him. He suppressed a grin at the momentary flash of annoyance on her face. Then he put in a controversial comment about the rapper 50 Cent and used the resulting distraction in the form of arguments from the group to give him time to watch Vanessa ditch the Latino guy and make her way across the room.

Annika waved to Vanessa as she approached, then introduced Vanessa to her friends. When she presented Cody, Vanessa explained casually that she already knew Cody and that he was doing some of her photo shots, too.

Annika put a possessive hand on Cody's arm. "We're going up to my condo in a little bit to socialize," she announced. "Want to come? You can bring a date."

Speculation lit Vanessa's eyes. Cody wondered if she thought she was being invited to a wild party or an orgy.

Vanessa inclined her head. "Sure, I'll tag along. I'll stop by my place on the way and get some champagne."

As the group chatted about vacations, the Latino man wandered over. Vanessa had her date.

After a while, the crowd started to thin and then the group left for Annika's condo. Along the way, Annika's friends found companions and reduced the ratio of men and women to half and half.

Annika's condo was built pretty much like Vanessa's, but the colors and the furniture were different. Annika's condo had lacquered Asian furniture and splashes of red throughout. Chinese rugs covered most of the hardwood floor in each room she passed.

Everyone sat in the entertainment room, which also served as the living room and dining room. Annika had used room service to order more appetizers. She drew several bottles of wine from a rack on the counter area in the kitchen. Vanessa placed her bottle of Crystal champagne with the others. The bar in the entertainment room was stocked with virtually everything else.

With a charming Spanish accent, Estevan, the criminal lawyer she'd met downstairs spoke to Vanessa about his legal exploits. One of his clients was big in the Mafia and was on trial for ordering a hit on a rival. What began as an interesting conversation turned boring as he began to repeat himself. Vanessa tried to change the subject, but he only wanted to talk about himself.

Several exchanges were going on at once. One couple was openly making out in a corner of the room, another couple was out on the terrace, smoking a joint. When Estevan palmed Vanessa's breast and tried to put his tongue down her throat, she pushed him away and asked him to take it slow. Two minutes later he was grabbing her ass as she reached for her glass. She lost it—one backward jab of her elbow to his chest and he was coughing and gasping for breath.

"Would you like some water?" she asked in a

voice made to sound concerned. She was glad when
Estevan declined and left her to join the group out
on the terrace. Across the room, she caught Mackenzie watching her. He looked amused. Apparently
he'd seen the whole thing.

Scanning the room, she saw that everyone was
engaged one way or another. It was the perfect time
to check Annika's condo. She stood and casually
walked to the kitchen.

The room had been decorated in the zen fusion
style, which Vanessa remembered meant beautiful
materials simply used to transmute the ordinary into
quiet grace. There was a stainless-steel refrigerator,
matching stainless steel oven and a hardwood floor.
Dark granite covered the counters.

Opening a honey-colored hardwood cabinet, Vanessa scanned the contents. It was filled with straw-
berry, vanilla and chocolate diet drinks, diet soda
and enough powdered shake mix to last a month. Vanessa understood what she was looking at; she'd
gone to the grocery store this morning and now her
own cupboards looked like Annika's.

The opposite kitchen cabinet was filled with
every kind of vitamin imaginable, as well as a number of diet drugs and medicines to clean out the
body. So far nothing seemed unusual.

Reaching up, Vanessa opened the small center

cabinet and stared. Front and center among the spices was a clear glass bottle with a label that read "Caribbean Mama Spice Mix."

Her pulse sped up and she suddenly felt hot and sweaty despite the air-conditioned room. She tore off a sheet of paper towel and, securing the bottle, opened it and poured about half a teaspoonful on to the paper towel. It certainly looked like spice. Folding it carefully into a packet, she slipped it into the pocket of her jeans. Then she closed the jar. As she placed it back in the cabinet, she heard a noise behind her.

"What *are* you doing?" someone asked in an indignant voice.

Startled, Vanessa shrieked. The cabinet banged shut. She turned to find Annika standing in the kitchen doorway, glaring at her.

Chapter 5

Bending over and trying to think fast, Vanessa held her chest. How much had Annika seen? Vanessa's heart was pounding so loud she could barely hear.

"What are you doing?" Annika repeated. Her voice increasing in volume and sounded testy.

"You scared me!" Vanessa gasped, straightening. She added a convincing giggle. Better to be considered a dingbat than a thief or a DEA agent. "I was looking for the coffee. I need something strong to cut through this buzz."

Annika stared at her for a moment and then up at the cabinet, which was now closed. Her eyes narrowed. She looked at Vanessa as if she wasn't sure she believed her.

"The coffee?" Vanessa prompted, boldly meeting her gaze.

"Oh. It's in the center canister over there," Annika said, pointing to a row of stainless-steel canisters.

Vanessa opened the canister and the rich scent of premium coffee filled her nostrils. She drew out the scoop.

"Do you need help with anything?" Mackenzie was standing in the doorway looking concerned.

About time, Vanessa fumed inwardly. He could have stopped Annika from finding her in the kitchen.

"Uh, Vanessa's making coffee," Annika said. Taking a step toward Mackenzie, she turned back to face Vanessa. "Can you handle it on your own?"

"Sure," Vanessa lied. She still felt a little shaky over getting caught at Annika's cabinet. She'd never made coffee in her life, but wasn't about to admit that. Could it be that hard?

Mackenzie called out as Annika led him away, "About two tablespoons per cup—"

Annika cut him off. "I use a little more than that. Oh, she knows what to do."

How much was "a little more than that"? At a

loss, Vanessa decided to use three tablespoons per cup in the automatic coffeemaker. She forgot the filter, so she found a metal strainer in the drawer and strained the grounds out of the finished brew. The coffee was so strong that no amount of cream changed the dark-chocolate color. Ugh! After one experimental taste, she tossed her drink down the sink.

In the entertainment room, she discovered that some of the couples had already left, and she was thankful that Estevan was gone, too. Annika sat on Mackenzie's lap, fingering his neatly trimmed hair. Was he working or was he enjoying himself with Annika? Somehow Vanessa didn't think Annika was his type.

Vanessa cleared her throat. Annika glanced up, a dazed expression in her eyes. Mackenzie's dark eyes were luminous, but he seemed to be in control of the situation. Vanessa guessed that he was working after all. "I've got to go. I had a great time. Thanks for having me," she said politely.

"Sure. Come back again, sometime." Annika was already turning back to Mackenzie.

Vanessa was glad to get back home. In her condo kitchen, she found a magnifying glass, opened her packet and examined the small mound of white powder she'd taken from Annika's kitchen.

It didn't take long to realize that she didn't know what she was looking for. For someone who'd known the powder too intimately in the past, she felt inadequate.

One thing was certain. The supposed spice had no odor. In movies and television shows she'd watched, people tasted the suspect powder on a moistened fingertip to determine if it was in fact cocaine. Vanessa's mouth watered. She didn't dare: she knew where that road led. Her hands trembling, she closed the packet and put it away.

An hour later, someone rang her doorbell. Upstairs, Vanessa stopped moisturizing her arms and legs to check the monitor. She recognized Mackenzie's face and went down to answer the door.

Mackenzie's gaze lingered for a second on her bare legs in short shorts. "I just left Annika's," he said, stating the obvious as he followed her into the kitchen. "Were you searching her kitchen?"

"Yeah. Thanks for keeping her out," she said, sarcasm creeping into her tone.

"I'd have done a better job if you'd told me what you were planning."

Vanessa nodded. "Fine. Sorry. I should have told you."

Acknowledging her apology with a nod of his own, he said, "Could have, would have, should have.

I should have figured out what you were doing a little sooner. It's been some time since I worked with a partner, so I'm a little rusty. And there's the fact that we're still getting to know each other." He extended a hand. "Truce?"

"Yes, let's call a truce." She shook hands with him.

Drawing a chair away from the kitchen table, he dropped down into it. "Did you find anything?

She retrieved the package and showed him the mound of powder.

He examined the powder carefully and refolded the paper towel. "Where'd you find it?"

"In a Caribbean Mama Spice Mix container in her kitchen cabinet. I didn't dare take the whole thing."

He put the folded packet into his pocket. "I don't know what this powder is, but that was good work and quick thinking. I'll take it to the lab and have it analyzed tomorrow."

Vanessa took the chair next to him, suddenly feeling exhausted from today's photo shoot and the party. "So, how long will it take?"

"A day or so. It really depends on how busy they are. I think I got a few leads myself."

"Mmm-hmm." She scooted closer, glad that they were finally starting to act like a team.

"When she went to freshen up, I went through her address book and found Gena and Bianca's names and numbers. I took pictures of the rest of the pages."

Vanessa wondered if he'd slept with Annika, though, it really wasn't any of her business. She gave him a speculative look.

As if he'd read her thoughts, Mackenzie chuckled and said, "I don't get paid to sleep with the suspects, Vanessa. That's not how we operate."

"We're checking all the names and numbers in her address book for drug connections?" she asked, changing the subject.

He nodded. "Yes. We'll run everything through the police and FBI databases and go from there."

Vanessa stifled a yawn.

Obviously taking it as a hint, Mackenzie stood. "You should get some sleep. We're going to start shooting at the Whitelaw Hotel over on Collins Avenue at seven o'clock. You could walk over there from here."

Saying her goodbye, Vanessa stood and stretched. As she saw him out, she was already thinking about the work she would be doing in the morning. It could be grueling if the weather didn't cooperate.

Barefaced and barely awake, with her gold-streaked hair up in a ponytail, Vanessa walked into the ultramodern lobby of the Whitelaw the next morning. She felt a little uncomfortable, and despite tea and a slice of raisin toast, she was nursing a nervous stomach. She didn't feel like a supermodel. She simply knew her flaws and was good at minimizing them.

One of Keifer Jonas's assistants was waiting to sign her in and get her connected with wardrobe, hair and makeup. A few minutes later in a private room, she looked over the number of suits that had been selected for her. There was a JETS Blue brand bikini in a pink, magenta, black and white design; a halter-topped, high-cut black Pilpel Hearts bikini, an artsy-looking black and white Vitamin A pop paisley bikini, and a retro-inspired, pastel-striped Sauvage Bardot bikini. All were designs she knew would highlight her generous breasts, small waist and curvy hips.

The big, red-haired, green-eyed Keifer Jonas hugged and kissed Vanessa and thanked her for accepting the assignment. She'd been at the top of both his and the magazine's wish lists.

By a quarter to seven a.m., she'd been through hair and makeup, and was dressed in the pop paisley number. While she waited for Keifer to get the set just right, she chatted with Savannah, another of the models.

Savannah's short, streamlined black hair, creamy white skin and vivid blue eyes provided a good contrast to Vanessa with her long, gold-streaked mane, hazel eyes and golden brown skin. Savannah wore a black and white polka-dot ruffle bikini by Liza Lozano. At nineteen, Savannah was on her way up in the modeling business. She'd already been on the covers of *Chic* and *Cosmopolitan*.

Looking at Savannah and taking in her youth, beauty and enthusiasm, Vanessa felt something lacking within herself. When she'd first gotten into modeling, she'd been young and idealistic and she'd had high hopes for her life and her career. That was more than a decade ago. Only twenty-seven years old now, she felt jaded.

Vanessa talked about being back in modeling after a two-year absence and dealing with a new world with a lot of friends gone. Luckily, she knew Keifer from her early modeling days, but the rest of the staff, models and publicity people were new to her. Savannah was sympathetic and gave Vanessa kudos for coming back to the business with a bang by landing a coveted contract with *Inside Sports*.

At seven sharp, Keifer was ready for them. Relaxing ambient music played as he posed Vanessa with her head back and one knee up on one of the white couches in front of a glass table covered with strategically placed sand and shells in the hotel's lobby. He'd added a black roll pillow to the other end of couch. Taking Savannah by the hand, he posed her on the short, round, column cushions, with one foot on the black carpeting and the other at an angle. Then he readjusted the light and began to take pictures, frequently changing each model's pose and moving her to a different area of the room. He took pictures of Vanessa alone while Savannah changed into another suit and vice versa. They worked for an hour before taking a break.

Keifer's assistant then drove everyone down to the beach, where Mackenzie was photographing models. He'd found a picturesque area with lush greenery and a backdrop of the art deco hotels. Observing him, Vanessa was impressed by his ability to get unique shots of each model.

Inside the beach cabana the models were using to change, Vanessa and Savannah walked in on two swimsuit models doing lines of coke. Vanessa knew that some models used it not only to get high, but also as a way to stay thin, since it decreased their appetite. If caught, they could be fired.

Savannah ignored them and went to the other side of the room to change. Transfixed, Vanessa stared for a moment, caught up in a mental image of her past. Her stomach tightened and her mouth turned dry as dust. She remembered the exhilaration and the feeling of great energy the drug gave. She'd felt she could do anything.

One of the other models noticed her watching and smiled. "Want some?"

"No." Vanessa forced herself to add, "Not right now." She turned away and began to undress. As she stepped out of her jeans and placed them on a chair, she couldn't get the image of the cocaine out of her mind. Her knees were shaking. Saying no had been harder than she'd imagined.

Changed into the pastel-striped Sauvage Bardot bikini, Vanessa left the cabana. As she sat in a lounge chair, the makeup artist modified her makeup to go with the outdoor lighting and oiled her skin. Then the stylist combed and teased her hair into a wilder, more leonine look.

Mackenzie divided his attention between her and his setup as he decided on which shots to take. Finally he positioned her so that she was lying partially in the water. The crew used buckets of water to wet the suit and cause water to bead up on Vanessa's skin. Despite the humidity, the suit dried time and time again and they had to wet her up frequently.

Vanessa felt like a drowned rat. This was the not-fun part of modeling. Her jaws ached so much from smiling that she was glad to switch back to a more seductive look.

When the session was finally over, Mackenzie helped her to her feet. She was hot, tired and covered with fine sand. Looking sexy was the last thing on her mind. The hint of banked heat she saw in his eyes caught her by surprise.

As she rinsed off the sand beneath the cold spray of the public shower on the beach, Vanessa saw that Savannah, who was still posing, was nearly done with her session, too. Vanessa lingered with a juice, ambling into the cabana at about the same Savannah did.

As they changed, Vanessa learned that Savannah was from Detroit and had been discovered during a model search at a local mall. She'd started with hopes of using the money for college and had stayed when the money quickly became more than she could even hope to make with a degree.

Vanessa mentioned starting out with Gena and how sad she was that Gena wasn't here to do the magazine shoot. That's when she discovered that Savannah had also known Gena. The woman's eyes sparkled as she talked of the lavish parties Gena had gotten her into.

With casual, careful questions and gentle leading,

Vanessa coaxed from Savannah the names of various people in the music, entertainment and publishing businesses who had thrown the parties. None rang a bell until Savannah bragged about having been to the home of hip-hop music mogul Taye Rollins at least twice.

Taye Rollins, aka Hot T, was the bad-boy-gone-good from a Miami street gang. Vanessa couldn't quite believe that the man would risk his reputation and all his hard work for drugs, but it was apparently something celebrities did every day. From having read the file Renee had given her, Vanessa knew that a lot of crime went on under the guise of the party scene.

Vanessa gathered her things. "You know, until I learn this city and meet some more people, my nights are pretty tame." She put a bit of a challenge in her gaze. "Think you could get me into one of Hot T's parties?"

Savannah hesitated, her fingers working the strap on her bag. Despite her talk of the party scene and having met the man, she didn't seem confident. "I…I could make sure you get a chance to meet him," she said.

Vanessa flashed her a brilliant smile. "Cool. I'd *love* to meet him."

Chapter 6

At the insistent ring of the phone, Vanessa jerked herself awake. Checking the clock, she saw that it was nearly six o'clock. She'd slept four hours straight. Her stomach growled noisily as she lifted the receiver and heard Mackenzie's voice.

"Let's meet for dinner," he suggested in a mellow tone that she hadn't heard from him previously.

No matter how much she tried to ignore it, there was some sort of connection between her and Cody Mackenzie. A grudging respect and a mild attraction? Vanessa wasn't sure she wanted to acknowledge it. If he could get over his problem with working with her, she saw him as someone she could be friends with.

"Business or pleasure?" she asked, wanting to make the ground rules clear.

"Business." His voice implied something altogether different. "But we can make it pleasant, if not downright pleasurable."

"Fine," she replied, wanting to ask him why he was acting differently toward her. "I've got business to discuss, too. Where do you want to meet?"

He named a bistro two blocks from her condo and Vanessa agreed to meet him there. As she changed into a Dolce & Gabbana denim dress with double-spaghetti straps and added denim slides, she justified her effort with the thought that she wasn't dressing for him. Her appearance was important to her job.

They arrived at about the same time and walked into the busy place together. Once seated at a little table along the back wall, Vanessa drank iced tea and told Mackenzie about her conversation with Savannah, and the discovery that Savannah had been friends with Gena.

Mackenzie's eyes lit up when Vanessa told him that Gena had gotten Savannah into music and entertainment parties, even some at Hot T's mansion.

"I heard the same thing from Rachel Warren, another model, this morning," he said.

"So you think we're onto something?" she asked.

"Yeah." His fingertips tapped the surface of the table as if he were playing an imaginary piano. "I've already started adding more to the Taye Rollins file. He used to be a member of the Street Killers."

Vanessa nodded. "I did an Internet search to find out more about him. I haven't read everything yet, but I'm working on it."

He scribbled into his notebook in what looked like code. "If you're covering the Internet and media angles, then I'll just concentrate on police and FBI records. Then we can compare notes."

"Sounds like a plan." Vanessa was encouraged that Mackenzie seemed to be showing her respect and treating her like a full partner. That funky little sneer he'd worn during their first meeting was no longer evident, either. She fell silent as the waiter brought their food and they began to eat.

Conscious of her weight, Vanessa ate only a quarter of the food on her plate and made up for it with a side salad. The food was decent, but not gourmet by any stretch of the imagination. They finished their meal in companionable silence. It provided a contrast to the various conversations going on around them, some rowdy or celebratory, others the typical banter of people on dates trying to impress one another.

"I put a rush on the analysis of the powder you got from Annika's," Cody said between bites. "I've got a friend in the lab. I felt like a fool when the analysis showed that it contained only spices."

"Oh no," Vanessa said in frustration.

"It's not your fault," Cody said quickly. "There's no way you could have known."

No way she could have known unless she'd tasted the powder. She knew how the real thing was supposed to taste.

"Look, stuff like this happens all the time," he assured her. "In fact, sometimes a guilty person will set up something like that to expose an undercover officer."

Vanessa expelled the air in her lungs. "Do you think…?"

Mackenzie shook his head. "No, I don't think Annika set you up, and she doesn't seem to suspect a thing. Maybe her using that spice jar was a coincidence."

"I don't really believe in coincidences," she confided.

Mackenzie didn't bother to reply, so she let the subject drop.

Sitting across from him, Vanessa still felt something she couldn't define. He wasn't trying to seduce or impress her, but each time their gazes met, she gritted her teeth. It was as if she were waiting for…something. But what?

She'd been enjoying a boyfriend break ever since she'd dropped Clayton Mercer III, the Mercer Aerospace Company heir. She and Clayton had been close friends since their days at The Dalton School and she'd gotten along famously with his family, until Clayton decided that he wanted her to be his girlfriend.

Clayton was sweet and she loved him dearly, but Vanessa suspected that beneath the hurt and dismay Clayton had shown when she broke up with him, he was somewhat relieved. No one in his family had ever dated a person of color, much less married one. Her crowning achievement in the entire affair was the fact that they were still friends.

"If you can find out who's on the inside of the party circuit, maybe you can get us into one of the parties at Hot T's," Mackenzie suggested once they'd ordered dessert. He was leaning across the table.

"I'm on it," Vanessa said coolly.

"What's your deal, Vanessa? What do you get out of doing this kind of work? Why aren't you on the charity circuit instead?"

"I *am* on the charity circuit," she snapped. "Ever hear of the Golden Key Foundation for Battered

Women? I'm one of the founders and a major supporter."

"What do you know about battered women?"

She blinked. "You'd be surprised." While modeling, she'd nearly lost a dear friend at the hands of an abusive boyfriend. It had affected her deeply, but she wasn't about to tell Mackenzie that. She didn't owe him an explanation.

"So why do you do this?" he asked again, referring to her work with the undercover organization.

"Because I *can.*" She slapped her palm on the table. "And because I'm good at it. Look at me. Most people look at me and all they see is eye candy. When they hear that my parents have a lot of money, it only adds to the fantasy." Gathering herself, she straightened her shoulders. "There's a lot more to me than my appearance and my parents' net worth."

He took that in, considered it, and then looked surprised. "All that is actually a sort of camouflage for you, isn't it?"

His question was so accurate that she let her lips curve into a smile. He'd actually listened and understood her.

"So, are you dangerous?" he asked in a husky tone.

"Very." Her voice dipped low, too.

"Dangerous women have always fascinated me,"

he said. He grasped her hand in his and massaged her fingers.

"Just as long as they don't aspire to be your partner, huh?" she asked, determined to call him on his attitude.

"Remember, I'm not used to working with a partner," he admitted, trying to weasel out.

"I'm not, either," she quipped, letting a bit of a challenge creep into her voice.

"Maybe some of us take longer to get used to it than others," he added in a backhanded apology.

"Obviously." Vanessa wasn't quite ready to let it go yet.

He pressed the issue. "So, are your initial impressions going to keep us from becoming friends?"

Vanessa shrugged. "I haven't decided yet, but I'm not usually one to hold grudges."

His fingers smoothed the back of her hand in long, sensuous strokes. "C'mon, Vanessa. You've shown me that you're up to the job and that you're not going to wait to ask for permission to get it done. We're equals. Let's not hold a grudge."

When they were done, Mackenzie walked her to her car.

"So, tell me more about why you do this job," she said.

His expression grew somber. "I grew up poor," he said, "but it was my mother's choice. She found out that my dad was a bigwig in a drug cartel. It nearly killed her, but she left him and took me with her. We spent years running and hiding from him."

"Where is your mother now?" she asked.

"She remarried. Now she lives in Chicago."

That left the obvious. "What about your dad?"

"He's dead. He was killed in a drug bust more than ten years ago."

Vanessa leaned against her car. "Are you making amends for the things he did?" she asked, picking her way carefully.

"Sort of." He nodded. "My mother gave me a strong sense of right and wrong. I'm a good agent and I've helped bring down some powerful drug gangs. I plan to do a lot more before I'm done with the MFD."

"That's admirable." Vanessa's voice softened. Somehow what he'd said made her feel closer to him.

"I'm not a saint," he insisted.

"I'd settle for a good partner right about now," she murmured, offering him her hand.

After hesitating almost imperceptibly, he accepted her hand and shook it firmly. "If that's the way you want to play it."

"It is," she said, hoping she'd made herself clear.

The only thing she wanted from Cody Mackenzie was backup and support on her assignment. Though, that didn't mean she couldn't enjoy the view or a little banter every now and then.

Chapter 7

After the scheduled photo sessions for the week were done, Vanessa got a surprise when Savannah called her to go nightclubbing with a friend. She didn't have much time to get ready.

She missed her large custom closet with all the built-in technology that she used at home. Perusing the clothes in the barely adequate condo closet, she selected a short black Dolce & Gabbana cocktail dress that circled her body with rings of asymmetrical black buttons and emphasized her curves. She stepped into a bronze-colored pair of Jimmy Choos. Hurrying, she stuffed her essentials into a matching evening bag, combed and fluffed her hair until it hung in a cloud past her shoulders, and added her favorite diamond earrings. Then she went outside to meet Savannah.

The women picked Vanessa up at ten in a white Cadillac Escalade. Savannah was driving. Her red-haired friend, Rita, a catalog and brochure model, was in the front passenger seat.

As Vanessa eased into the back, she saw that the other women had decked themselves out in slinky cocktail dresses that exposed lots of skin. They were taking her to The Opium Garden. The name had Vanessa imagining all sorts of scenarios, but she kept them to herself.

When she'd checked the place out on the Internet, she discovered that it was a club on Collins Avenue. Most of the references she'd found mentioned open-air space, sexy dance music, scantily clad dancers and celebrities.

At the club, Vanessa's spirits sank when she saw the long line of people waiting to get in. Was any club worth standing in a line like that? Unconcerned, Savannah climbed out of the car and led them right up to the front of the line. The doorman apparently knew Savannah, because he moved aside to usher them in without her saying a word. Vanessa was flattered when he gave her a reverent nod as she followed the other women past him.

The inside of the club resembled an exotic garden with an Asian theme. Chinese lanterns in red and white, towering palm trees and golden Buddha statues dotted the landscape. The place was huge. Long, contemporary style couches in red, black, indigo and tan filled various rooms. Heavy bass vibrated in the air, accentuating the sensual music. Instead of merely walking, Vanessa danced a little as they followed the hostess to their table.

Taking in the striking surroundings and swaying to the music, they ordered drinks. Savannah discreetly pointed out several celebrities seated around them. On her own, Vanessa recognized Nicole Ritchie, movie producer Benton Lansing and singer Mya. Some celebrities dotted the dance floor, shaking and twisting, undulating, and bouncing in the colorful crowd. The club was a place to people watch and be seen.

When the waitress appeared, they ordered wine, and as Vanessa sipped hers, men who obviously knew her two companions asked them to dance. For a while she watched them, comparing the colorful styles in Miami to the more conservative styles she usually saw in New York. Then she scanned the club impatiently. It didn't seem like the sort of place where a girl could or should dance alone.

Knowing that Benton Lansing was on the DEA list of suspects, she toyed briefly with the idea of wandering over to his table to introduce herself.

She sat alone at the table, an apparent wallflower for one of the few times in her life. It wasn't the first time she'd felt like the odd piece in a puzzle where everyone else fit. She'd made a place for herself with her classmates growing up and also with the models she'd started with, but all had been precarious positions. Fitting in had required that she suppress some parts of herself. With one group she kept slang and cultural references and experiences to a minimum, and with the other, kept her interactions focused on the modeling life, and her goals and struggles private. Even getting along with her parents required that she pass on some things she wanted to say or do.

She'd all but given up on the idea of dancing, when an attractive man in a white Armani suit with rolled-cuff baggy pants, a black silk tie and hanky, white shirt and dark glasses approached the table with all the presence and style of a male runway model. He extended a hand.

"Hey, I'm Taye. Want to dance?"

Recognizing Taye Rollins's killer smile, Vanessa

stood, returned the smile and took his hand. An electric current shot through her at the contact. Vanessa recoiled a little in surprise, but he held on to her hand. Mama mia, was that static electricity or did the man have that much charisma? "Vanessa, and I'd love to dance," she managed to say a little breathlessly.

He didn't let go of her hand until they were out on the dance floor. Then he began to move with a fluid grace and skill that Vanessa answered with her own sinuous dance. Their styles complemented each other. She was actually enjoying herself. Each time their glances met and held, she felt a pull toward him. He barely touched her again, but he danced close inside her personal space. She felt the heat of his body and a tingling across the surface of her skin. At times, he was close enough to kiss. There was no doubt that Taye Rollins was a sensuous man.

Reining in her thoughts, she reminded herself that he was a suspect. She had a job to do, and letting Taye Rollins find his way into her La Perla lingerie wasn't an option. Since he was attracted to her, she should be using that attraction to get close enough to him to investigate.

The thought of getting close to Taye warmed her insides. Her mouth felt dry. Vanessa wet her lips and saw his eyes darken. They'd barely spoken and yet he was affecting her on a level she'd never experienced with any other man.

The music ended and Vanessa toyed with the idea of returning to her table. Taye thanked her and offered his hand again.

"Another dance, Vanessa?"

She liked the sound of her name on his lips. It came out like a caress. And how could she not return that smile? She gave him her hand.

As a salsa tune began, he drew her into his arms and began a series of quick steps. All around them, couples were dancing. In the middle of the first awkward spin, Vanessa teetered in her heels and nearly lost her balance. He caught her easily, but heat rushed her face as she realized that this wasn't something she could bluff her way through. She told him that she didn't know how to salsa. She'd gone from graceful to gawky.

Looking surprised, Taye asked her if she wanted to try something else. Embarrassed, she wanted only to get off the dance floor.

Alone at the table once more, she watched Taye dip, step and spin a beautiful Latina woman in a thin white slip-dress, and resigned herself to having blown an opportunity. But two dances later, Taye came back to get her for a slow dance with a deep, grinding beat.

"Want to try a slow dance, Vanessa?" he asked, extending his hand.

Taking it, she swallowed her pride to follow him back to the crowd of dancers.

"I'm one of your greatest fans," he murmured as she settled in his arms.

"You are?" Vanessa breathed in the heady scents of expensive male cologne and the man himself. He could have bottled and sold it. Through the thin material of her dress, she felt the warmth of his fingers at her waist. One of her hands rested on his muscular biceps and the other clasped his big hand. She fought the urge to close her eyes.

"Oh yeah." He laughed softly. "I've got every one of your Sweetheart Dreams Catalogs. I've also got all your covers and the magazine spreads."

Her mouth curved up into a smile. "Do you have the spread I did for *Obsession Magazine,* too?" She couldn't help asking. It was the edgiest, sexiest thing she'd ever done because it pushed the limits between modeling and pinup centerfolds. The magazine had sold out, but her father had been so livid that he'd cut off her family allowance—again.

"Now that's my all-time favorite," Taye declared. "I actually have five copies of that one." His eyes sparkled. "Vanessa, you are one hot lady."

Taye Rollins was a hot one, too. She managed to

thank him and tell him that she had his *Stripped,
Ripped, Party, Greatest Hits* and *Thoughts* CDs.

"Then we're mutual fans," he said, moving her
smoothly across the floor.

Vanessa nodded.

"So are you free this evening?" he asked as the
music stopped. He stepped closer.

She felt hot and thirsty. Her feet were threatening to complain and Vanessa knew she wasn't up to
another dance.

"It depends on what you have in mind." Vanessa
dropped her arms. She was thrilled, but this was as
far as things were going.

He flashed her a smile. "I've got a table in the
corner over there with some of my friends. Want to
sit with us?"

How could she refuse? It was an opportunity to
get in with Taye and his friends. Vanessa found Savannah and told her where she'd be, then followed
Taye to his table.

Taye's friends actually filled two tables. They
were a loud, boisterous group of rappers, hip-hop
artists, wannabes and groupies. There were several
beautiful women. The men warmly welcomed Vanessa; the women were cool but polite. Vanessa
couldn't blame them—there were more women than
men and Taye Rollins was definitely the prize.

He introduced her to everyone and she recognized and cataloged several of the names. One of the other women asked her questions about the modeling business.

Taye moved around and spent time talking to everyone. Listening in on some of the conversations, Vanessa saw that he was mixing business with pleasure. Four of the men were members of a new rap/hip-hop group Taye was sponsoring. Two others worked for his record label. One of the women was an executive assistant there. No matter what the relationship, it was obvious that Taye was king here in the group. He wasn't autocratic, he was cool, calm and on top of things.

Another man at the table drawing a lot of attention and respect was the roughly attractive Jerrell Vaughn, one of Taye's record company executives. He stood out in the group with dark-chocolate-colored skin, a bald head and bedroom eyes. He didn't say much, but his sharp glances seemed to miss little. A couple of times Vanessa wondered if people were afraid of him. Then he smiled and made her question her instincts.

As it grew late, Savannah and Rita came to tell Vanessa that they were ready to go. After introducing the two to Taye's crowd, she stood, gathering her things and saying her goodbyes. Taye stood, too, and offered to take her home in his limousine in an hour or two. Vanessa was tired, so she declined and thanked him anyway.

When Taye asked for her number, Vanessa was excited, for more reasons than one. She reached into her evening bag and gave him one of her personal cards. He walked her to the door, and as she stood at the entrance with him, she anticipated some sort of gesture—but what? His lips looked inviting, but he didn't know her well enough to kiss her. Surprising her, he lifted her hands and pressed a warm kiss on each.

"I'm looking forward to seeing you again," he said.

"I am, too," she admitted.

He walked her out to the car and helped her in. With a squeeze of her hand and a murmured good-bye, he was gone.

"Woo-ee! You finally met Taye. How'd you pick him up?" Savannah asked as they drove off.

Laughing, Vanessa explained what had happened. Her thoughts lingered on the man. She'd sensed something real behind his smooth, easygoing manner. She wanted him to call, but at the same time hoped he wouldn't. With her luck, he was probably a bona fide member of the drug ring and she'd be getting close to him only to send him off to prison.

"I was sort of wishing I'd stayed at the table," Rita laughed.

They had gone a mile or so up the avenue when Savannah decided that she just had to have a soda. Turning at a busy intersection, she drove a few blocks and pulled into the parking lot of a convenience store.

Alarm bells went off in Vanessa's head when she got a good look at the neighborhood. It was rough. She felt edgy when Savannah brushed off her suggestion that they find another store.

No other customers were inside the building and as they stood at the counter to pay, Vanessa began to relax. Then a noisy group of guys in jeans, shorts, tank tops and T-shirts entered the store. Some of them were drunk or high. They were rowdy as they eyed the women and made rude and lewd comments just loud enough to be heard. Under their scrutiny, Savannah adjusted her dress. Vanessa wished she'd worn a wrap.

"Go quickly," the man behind the counter urged them under his breath.

Glancing back at the men, Savannah and Rita looked frightened.

Vanessa fought to keep her cool. She would be okay as long as no one drew a gun. "Go on. I'll pay for the sodas and meet you at the car," she told Savannah and Rita in a hushed voice. "Hurry up and get it started."

The men opened a small space to let the women pass. Then they closed in on Vanessa. She did her best to remain calm. Accepting her change from the clerk, she put it in her purse and snapped it closed. Then she lifted the bag of sodas into her arms.

Vanessa turned to see the four guys standing there. She didn't like the odds. She'd been trained, yeah, but she wasn't superhuman. She ran through various scenarios in her head—all of them ended with her fighting. She took a step.

The men didn't part to let her pass. The blond surfer boy with the wild-looking hair puffed out his chest and gave her the eye. "Hey, sweet cheeks, got some time for some real men?"

"I would if there was a real man standing here." The words were out of her mouth before she even thought about them. Vanessa clamped her jaw shut. Those were fighting words.

"Bitch!" A wiry man in a blue muscle shirt used his wide shoulders to push his way to the front of his friends. "You wouldn't know a real man if he bit you in the ass!"

She'd have liked to see a real man *try*. Vanessa swallowed hard. She wasn't usually so cocky and she wasn't dressed for a fight. Yeah, she'd learned to fight in her stilettos, but it required concentration and balance. Why hadn't she kept her big mouth shut? She decided to let Blue Muscle Shirt's comment about not knowing a real man pass.

"Maybe not, but I don't want any trouble. Can you let me by?"

"I think we should teach her a lesson," the dark-haired one in the black tank said with a laugh.

"You think you're bad enough to take us, bitch?"

Vanessa met that challenging stare without blinking. She wasn't planning on backing down because she knew that with any sign of weakness on her part, they'd be on her in seconds. Keeping her mouth shut was one of the hardest things she'd ever done.

"Let her go or I'm calling the police," the clerk behind the counter yelled. He lifted the phone to dial.

"I don't think so," surfer boy jeered. Two guys in white T-shirts were on the clerk in a flash, wrestling the phone from his hands and roughly pushing him down to a sitting position on the floor in front of the counter.

Vanessa wondered if he'd had time to push the silent alarm. Surely there was one? In any case, the fight was on—whether they knew it or not. Scanning the men, she weighed her options as she waited for them to make their move.

The wiry one grabbed her by the arm hard

enough to bruise. A rush of adrenaline replaced the tightness in her chest.

Vanessa lifted the cans of soda and swung. With a loud *thack,* the cans hit him with enough force to send him reeling backward. She followed it up with a stiletto-heeled kick to his crotch.

Yowling in pain, he curled into a ball on the floor.

Fists and elbows flying furiously, she whirled and met surfer boy and his husky, frog-eyed friend with powerful blows. They *were* drunk she decided, as they went down in an uncoordinated tangle.

The two men holding the clerk were the only two left standing. They glanced from the two men bent on regaining their feet, to Vanessa. Before they could come to a decision, Vanessa did the smart thing and ran for the exit.

"Hey!" someone yelled after her.

Catching sight of the broom near the door, she grabbed it and kept going. Outside in the store's parking lot, Savannah had the car running. The rear passenger door was open and waiting for Vanessa.

She was nearly there when her right heel hit a crack in the pavement. Shifting her weight, it took everything she had to keep from twisting her ankle. Beneath the stress, the heel of her shoe broke. She felt it as keenly as if she'd broken her arm or leg; they were a pair of her favorite shoes.

At the sound of running footsteps on the pavement, she scrambled to her feet, swinging the broom like it was a fighting stick. It smacked the guy in the head. As he reeled, the others watched her from a distance, yelling obscenities.

Vanessa hobbled the rest of the way to the car, then tossed the broom to the ground and got into the back seat. "Hurry up and get us out of here!" she yelled.

They'd gone several blocks before Savannah said, "I was worried about you. We shouldn't have left you alone in the store like that, no matter what you said. I'm glad you're all right."

"I used my cell phone to call the police," Rita said. "What did you do in there? It looked like you might have been fighting with those guys."

"They didn't want to let me go," Vanessa admitted. "I wasn't going to just stand there and let them hurt me."

Rita turned around in her seat to look at Vanessa. "Where'd you learn to fight? Were you in a gang?"

Vanessa's head came up and she met Rita's gaze. She guessed that Rita had preconceived notions about African Americans and thought she'd come up from the ghetto. Vanessa wanted to slap her.

"Rita, Vanessa is from Scarsdale! Her parents are the Dawsons that own all that real estate," Savannah put in quickly.

Rita blinked, looking as if she felt stupid.

Vanessa kept the anger out of her voice. "I took private lessons after I dropped an old boyfriend and he started stalking me." That was the truth, too, only what Vanessa had learned before was child's play compared to what Jimmy Valentine had taught her at the Gotham Rose Club.

"Oh." Rita looked embarrassed. She turned back in her seat to face the road.

The anger stayed with Vanessa as the car sped through the Miami streets. She'd managed to bring down a menacing bunch of guys. Would she be as successful when she found the group responsible for Gena and Bianca's murders?

Chapter 8

Vanessa slumped back in the seat. Some hero she was. She wasn't seriously hurt, but she felt battered and alone. Somehow she always ended up alone, physically, mentally or emotionally. Her arm throbbed and her hands were starting to swell. She thrust the poor-little-rich-girl thoughts out of her mind.

At the condo complex, she climbed out of the car holding her ruined shoes and said goodbye to the girls. The area was deserted. Even the complex's restaurant and club were closed. Barefoot, she picked her way to her unit on the warm ground. At the door she inserted her key and paused to look around. The back of her neck tingled, and she sensed that she was being watched. After a quick scan of the moonlit grounds, she opened the door and went inside.

The message light on her answering machine blinked furiously. She ignored it to plop down on her couch with a bowl of ice for her hands.

Three minutes later someone tapped on her door. Startled, she drew her gun from its hiding place in the ceiling tiles. It was going on two-thirty in the morning. She'd had more than enough excitement for one night. Gripping the cool metal with aching hands, she stared through the peephole. It was Mackenzie. With a sigh, she opened the door.

"Hi, you okay?" he asked, looking wary as he stepped into the room. "When you didn't check in, I called. Then I got worried. It's been hours."

She closed the door. Thankfully, she had nothing scheduled for the morning and could afford to stay up a little while longer.

He took in the gun, the bruise on her arm and her rumpled appearance. Then he surprised her with a sympathetic hand on her shoulder. "You okay? What happened?"

Motioning him to the chair, she dropped down on the sofa and told him.

"Savannah should have known better," he said angrily.

He made a quick survey of her bathroom cabinet and the kitchen and came back with a plastic bag filled with ice cubes, a roll of tape, a glass of water, and a couple of anti-inflammatory pain relievers. The throbbing in her arm eased when he taped the bag around it.

Mackenzie settled beside her on the sofa. "You've had a busy night. Besides the fight, you lucked out on Taye Rollins and his crew. So you really think he'll ask you out?"

Remembering the attraction between her and Taye, Vanessa nodded. "He walked me to the door and said that he would call." She didn't add that it was the oldest line in the book and one people used whether they meant it or not.

Mackenzie said that he'd called earlier because they had done some checking through police and agency databases and discovered that Annika had some drug-related arrests and used to belong to one of the gangs.

Suddenly more alert, Vanessa leaned forward. This could be one way of connecting some of the suspects. "Which gang?" she asked.

"Street Killers."

Her fingers curled into the bowl of ice. "Isn't that the gang Taye Rollins used to be in?"

Cody nodded. "Yeah, but most of the members in his age group quit when they hit eighteen."

"So you think it's just a coincidence that we're coming across members of that gang?"

He shot her a quelling glance. "I did *not* say that. I think we should start tracking the number of former Street Killers we can connect to Gena, Bianca and our drug-gang suspects. Maybe they are still working together."

Vanessa relaxed back into the sofa. "My thoughts exactly."

Long after Mackenzie went home, Vanessa sat on the couch thinking about Taye Rollins and the Street Killers. She knew that he was no angel, but when she'd been with him, thug was the last thing on her mind. Rumor had it that his bad-boy image was well deserved. Was that what she'd found so attractive?

She wished she could get a look at Taye's juvenile record to see just what he was capable of. Maybe it would take the edge off the attraction she felt. Maybe it wouldn't. Vanessa ruefully acknowledged her own hidden past. How could she condemn anyone?

Jerrell Vaughn's face came to mind and she shivered. Instincts warned her that he was the more treacherous of the two men. No matter what, she couldn't let her guard down. The game was on.

The next day, Mackenzie told Vanessa that due to persistent rumors of drug running, the DEA had wanted to get into Hector Guerra's design rooms and warehouse for a while, but had nothing concrete to go on. He asked Vanessa to try to get the intelligence on Guerra's security and he gave her a lotion-like fixative that could be used to pick up his hand-prints.

During the week, Vanessa applied makeup to the bruise on her arm and used her downtime to attend a Hector Guerra fashion show at his Miami location. It was a large, modern brick building in a trendy part of town. She and Mackenzie had agreed that she would be able to gather more information if he did not come along.

Having had her publicist call Guerra to inform him that she would be attending his show, Vanessa arrived early for a private tour. Guerra met her himself. Tall, with black, shiny hair that hung past his neck and beautiful dark eyes, he was a striking man. His pictures didn't do him justice. Taking her hand, he introduced himself and recalled his favorites among the outfits she'd modeled in the past.

Guerra's security was impressive. Vanessa knew

why: sometimes fashion designs and expensive materials were stolen before they were ever presented to the public. If Guerra was hiding something, few people had access to it. Security guards were everywhere, and he explained that his design and storage areas were protected with bio-scans of his most trusted and talented employees. Glad she'd coated her hands with a moist fixative that was already drying with Guerra's fingerprints, she watched as he placed his hands on a scanning plate outside the door.

The indicator light above the door turned green. She heard the lock click. Guerra opened the door on a workroom filled with colorful designs in progress. She fell in love with a fitted lime-green cotton dress with artistic black stripes for herself, and a pink silk blouse with gold stars for Michelle. Guerra promised to sell them to her at a discount after the show.

In the rear warehouse area of the facility, Guerra opened a few shipping containers and Vanessa glimpsed reams of gorgeous fabrics decorated with unique designs and trims. Scanning the transport labels, she noted that they were from all over the world. His fashion house could be the perfect cover for transporting drugs.

Guerra asked probing questions about her return to modeling and the reasons why she'd left. She tried to keep her answers oblique but truthful, but he persisted. Finally she told him that her reasons were something she didn't want to share.

"You should keep searching until you find what you're looking for," Guerra said as they headed back to the main part of his building.

Nerves abruptly tightening, she glanced at him. He acted as if he could see right through her. She wondered if he had somehow discovered that she was working with the DEA. "Are you referring to my modeling, or the show?" she asked, trying to focus his statement.

Dark eyes regarded her without revealing a thing. "I mean anywhere you're searching," he answered cryptically.

At a loss, she shrugged and thanked him. Maybe it had been just an innocent comment.

Minutes later, she struggled to hide her shock when they encountered Annika on the way back to the area where the staff was busy seating the audience for the show. She hadn't seen Annika since the incident in her kitchen.

In a yellow chiffon blouse that left nothing to the imagination, tight black pants and yellow slingbacks, Annika greeted them. Then she slipped into Guerra's arms and pressed herself against him for a showy kiss that included plenty of lip and tongue.

Annika and Guerra? Vanessa wondered if the couple had a connection other than the exchange of body fluids.

The kiss ended and they separated. "I see you've met Hector," Annika gushed, one proprietary arm still around his waist. Triumph glittered in her eyes. "He's a really good friend of mine."

Obviously. Vanessa acknowledged the comment with a slight incline of her head. She wanted to tell the woman that she didn't want him. And if things were so hot with Guerra, what had Annika been doing with Mackenzie?

Guerra left to make sure his staff had everything in order for the show, and an associate hustled Vanessa and Annika out to special guest seats near the front.

"How did you meet Hector?" Vanessa asked when they were settled.

"Oh, I've known him since we were kids," Annika replied.

Vanessa stifled a quick intake of breath. Kids? As in…neighborhood gang? She didn't ask, but she wondered if the couple had discussed her.

Cameras flashed continuously as the models walked the runway in Guerra's designs. It brought back memories for Vanessa. She'd walked the runway, too. The last year she'd done it, she'd been so high that it was a wonder she hadn't fallen flat on her face.

The crowd was receptive and rightly so. Guerra had created some of the most wearable designs available.

Afterward, Vanessa lingered to say hello to a few school friends who were vacationing down in Palm Beach. Seeing them made her a little homesick for New York and her sister Michelle. When she saw Rubi Cho moving her way, she ducked back into the crowd. The columnist seemed to be everywhere. Vanessa was damned if she'd give the woman any fodder for her column. Besides, the publicity could hurt the mission.

That evening, Vanessa met Mackenzie for dinner at a Mexican restaurant several blocks away from the complex. He made notes in a little black book while she went through the details of Guerra's security system. A separate team would be checking the premises soon.

She and Mackenzie discussed their progress on the assignment. Vanessa felt that they should have more to show for their efforts so far, but Mackenzie was satisfied. He spoke from experience and cautioned her that sometimes it took a long time to pull all the evidence together—other times you got lucky and it all came together unexpectedly.

They were finishing their dessert when he looked

up and asked, "Have you heard from Taye Rollins yet?"

She hated to admit she hadn't. It was hard to believe that she'd fallen for what had to be the oldest line in the book. Sitting at that table in the club with Taye and all those other women, Vanessa had thought she'd sensed something between them. Maybe she was losing her touch. Maybe she'd never had it to begin with.

Vanessa stopped mentally kicking herself. It wasn't as if she'd been pining away, waiting for Taye Rollins's call. She was trying to do her job. "If I haven't heard from him by the end of the week, I'll think of something," she promised.

"I bet you will," Mackenzie said.

Cody spent the next few days developing pictures and going over the shots he'd taken of the models on the beach. The ones he'd taken of Vanessa outshone all the rest. In most of her shots, there was little or no touch-up work to be done. She was a gorgeous woman, and with her innate sensuality, all her photos were quality.

When he first met Vanessa all he could see was her physical beauty, pedigree and bank account. Now she was his partner and he knew what a good and dedicated agent she was. They'd weathered a rocky start, sized each other up and worked their way to mutual respect.

Toward the end of the week, he was back on the beach, redoing some of the shots with the other models. He knew that Vanessa was still working the party angle and having limited success. Many of the models were unwilling to share their connections.

By Friday Vanessa was ready to work on getting her own invitation to Hot T's. She planned on using the hip-hop concert that night featuring Hot T, Nelly, and the ChiTown 7, to get in with Taye Rollins. Determined to make this work, she'd tagged Mackenzie for escort duty and had even tried to get into what he would wear. That's where he'd drawn the line. Yes, he'd probably be a little older than most of the crowd, but he knew how to dress. He'd been doing it for thirty-seven years without embarrassing himself.

As he donned an expensive white T-shirt with designer detailing and a black pair of Fubu jeans, he shook his head and bristled. Did ten or twelve years really make that much of a difference? *Hell, yeah.*

Checking himself in the mirror, Cody added a one-carat diamond earring and a couple of gold chains. Then he brushed and combed his hair and splashed on a little of his favorite cologne.

Vanessa showed up dressed for attention and

glowing in a beaded silk camisole in lime-green that was held up by thin straps that crossed in the back and dipped low between her breasts in the front. Camel-colored canvas slacks hugged every curve of her bottom and skimmed her long legs.

When she walked, she balanced easily on matching camel-colored stiletto slides that probably cost more than a month of his salary. Her hair was done Hollywood style with vertical curls that framed her face and covered much of her back. For the umpteenth time he looked at her, amazed all over again at how luminously beautiful she was. She was a nice girl, too, and deserved something and someone more than the glitzy but shallow characters he'd seen flocking around her. Too bad she wasn't interested in him.

"I like your outfit," she said.

Was she conceding that he could dress himself after all? Mackenzie threw her an I-can-see-through-your-bullshit look.

Vanessa broke into peals of musical laughter.

After a moment, he laughed, too, and returned the compliment.

"Do you like rap and hip-hop?" she asked as they settled into her car.

"It's cool," he responded. "How about you?"

She lifted a slim shoulder in a shrug. "It depends

on the artist and the cut. I do have some P. Diddy, Hot T, Nelly, Eminem and 50 Cent CDs. I've got a lot of Usher, too, but he's more rhythm and blues."

At the large amphitheater where the concert was being held, Vanessa made an unsuccessful attempt to see the hip-hop mogul backstage before the show. Her publicist had called in an attempt to arrange something beforehand, but Hot T's people had closed ranks on her. Taye probably didn't even know Vanessa would be there.

Glamorous as any movie star and not fazed by the brush-off, Vanessa led Mackenzie to their seats in the celebrity section near the stage. It was just as well, since the crowd was rowdy and Mackenzie didn't want to have to worry about protecting her, even if she could fight in stilettos. He scanned the group and did his best not to stare at the other celebrities. He spotted Lionel Ritchie with his daughter Nicole, Earvin "Magic" Johnson and a woman who looked like Janet Jackson.

Once the concert began, Vanessa stood up to dance and show her appreciation of the music every chance she got. When Taye Rollins took the stage, the crowd roared. Women in skimpy clothes bumped, grinded and danced around him and the band members as part of the show. Without some of the words being bleeped out the way they were on the radio, the language in the songs was pretty rough. The audience took it all in with enthusiasm and seemed ready for whatever the hip-hop groups could dish out.

Mackenzie knew the exact moment Hot T noticed Vanessa among the celebrity fans. The mogul gave her a long, hard look. During the next two numbers he focused on the crowd of fans, but his attention came back to Vanessa over and over again. By the time Hot T was ready to perform his last number, he'd personally asked Vanessa to join him on stage.

"We're on our way," she murmured under her breath. A radiant smile lit her face. "Wait for me here. I'll make sure he invites you, too."

Feeling a little uncomfortable, Cody agreed. Vanessa was taking point again and working it good. He wondered how Vanessa would explain him to Hot T. Then it dawned on Cody that the truth—that he was her photographer on the magazine shoot—would dispel any doubts Hot T might have about the situation.

On stage, Vanessa danced with Hot T while he rapped and sang to her. To her credit, she managed to look hot and sexy without mimicking the suggestively erotic moves of the professional dancers onstage. Taye Rollins appeared to be fascinated.

Cody stared, niggling concern growing. Vanessa wasn't acting. He hoped her hormones wouldn't get them both killed.

Chapter 9

Comfortably seated next to Taye Rollins in the back of the limousine, Vanessa breathed a sigh of relief when the entourage made room for Mackenzie. If things went as she hoped, he would help her get enough evidence to cross Taye Rollins off the DEA list of suspects.

She scanned the group, abruptly realizing how much it excited her just to be in their midst. She'd never gotten into being a groupie or chasing after movie or music stars, but somehow this was different. Taye Rollins might be bad-boy cool, but she sensed something she liked about the man behind the image.

In the group she recognized Jerrell Vaughn, the female executive assistant, and one of the rappers Taye was sponsoring.

Taye caught her hand, bringing her attention back to him. Pure pleasure flashed through her at his touch. His brown eyes exerted a strong pull that went deeper than their undeniable physical attraction. She wanted much more, and it scared her because she might well end up helping to put Taye Rollins away for a very long time.

Leaning close, he spoke in an intimate whisper. "I'm glad you turned up in tonight's audience."

"I am, too," she replied. When they had some semblance of privacy, she would bring him to task for not calling her. And then she would see what she could discover about Taye and any connections he might have to the drug gang, and the two dead models.

They rode in the limousine for quite a while. Not knowing a lot about Miami, she wasn't sure how much was actual travel time and how much was time spent losing anyone who might be following them.

Soon they were in a residential area. Down a secluded road a pair of iron gates opened outward and the car took the circular drive through exotic plants and palm trees to the front door of a long, white brick mansion. They piled out to be ushered past fancy white doors embellished with Taye's initials in gold. Treading plush white and gold carpets, they ended up in the party room, which was a large den in the east wing. Taye's gold and platinum records decorated one wall. Paintings of several rap, hip-hop, and rhythm and blues artists, performing live, covered the other walls.

Taye drew her to a red, leather Morrey couch and settled beside her. His butler appeared and took drink orders. As if on cue, selections from Taye's latest CD began to play in the background. The others took seats on the various couches, chairs and love seats around them. On the other side of the room, Vanessa saw Mackenzie talking with Taye's executive assistant.

Realizing that this was as close to private as she was going to get for the moment, Vanessa turned to give Taye her full attention. Their gazes locked.

Sensing something in her eyes, he held up one hand. "Please, let me go first. You're probably wondering why I didn't call…"

Smart man. Vanessa nodded. "It crossed my mind."

"The truth is that I've had a hell of a week. Some of the bookings we've done for Yo were cancelled and I had to personally pump 'em up and call in some markers to set them back on the schedule. Then the new material written for Playahs wasn't working out, so I put another team together and we sat down and wrote a whole new set of songs. On top of that, I've been looking for a new factory for my clothing line because the one we have now got sold and the new management is running a sweatshop. Then, the Dream Foundation had a last-minute request from a kid dying from cancer. I performed for him and spent a day with him at Disneyland. Do you need to hear more?"

Vanessa blinked. Taye was a very busy man. She wondered how any woman could figure prominently in his scheme of things. The part about the kid dying of cancer affected her most of all. It sounded like the ultimate sob story and yet it pulled at her heart. Did he make that up? And then, why should he? The man could have almost any woman he wanted, just by crooking his little finger.

"Is there more?" she asked in a light, even tone.

"Oh yeah." He flashed a smile. "But I'm still sorry I didn't call."

"It sounds like your week was action packed," she admitted. "I don't need to hear any more."

Their drinks arrived. She took a long sip and set the glass down, to find him watching her intensely.

He shifted his position. "So what did you do this week?"

She told him, patiently answering his questions about locations, the types of shots and the designers that had been chosen. His interest seemed genuine and she appreciated it.

"I've already told you that I'm a big fan," he said, his eyes warming. "Can I get a copy of your shooting schedule so I can come and watch?"

She laughed again. Yes, she'd heard that line before, but coming from Taye, it sounded sincere and meant more than from someone trying to get a thrill off seeing her in a photo shoot for *Inside Sports*. "I'll send you some autographed pictures," she promised.

He leaned closer—almost close enough for their lips to touch. "I want to take my own. Think about it."

"I will." Still smiling, she was beginning to wonder if he was interested only in her physical assets. Then he asked about the Golden Key Foundation. She could have fainted with the shock. Obviously, he followed her activities closely.

As she finished her drink, she noticed that several of the others had disappeared. Were they in Taye's guest rooms, getting busy and wearing out the sheets? At least eighty percent of the hip-hop music she'd heard involved having sex, thinking about it or getting ready for it, so her suspicion wasn't much of a stretch. Then again, maybe they'd gone on to party elsewhere. On the other side of the room, she saw that Mackenzie was still talking to the executive assistant.

Time to get down to business. "How about a tour?" she asked.

"Sure." Taye got up and led the way out of the room.

As they passed close to one of the walls covered with paintings, Vanessa stopped to read the signature on the bottom of one. Recognizing "Rollins," she whipped around to put a hand on his arm. "You painted these?"

"Yeah." He looked a little sheepish. "It's one of my hobbies, but I haven't gone public with it."

She examined the canvas in front of her. 50 Cent, Usher and several other artists were performing on a giant stage. She read the title on the metal plate at the bottom, "Lovers and Friends," and remembered the song. They'd all performed together on a CD by that name. "It's really good," she breathed.

"Think so?" He sounded pleased but there was no arrogance in his tone.

"You know it is," she insisted.

"Want it? I'll give it to you."

That startled her. She loved the painting, but it

had to be worth a lot. The fact that Taye Rollins had painted it only added to its value. "I—I couldn't accept it."

His tone took on an edge. "Why not? Do you really even like it?"

"Yes, I do," she said, emphasizing every word and making eye contact with him.

"Then take it. I'll have Smith wrap it up."

"Okay." She gave in, deciding that she would handle the guaranteed fallout coming her way from Renee and Mackenzie for accepting a gift from a suspect. "Can I pay for it? Give you something for all the work you've put into it?"

"Don't insult me," he muttered, moving on and leaving her to follow. "Still want that tour?"

"Yes." She hurried to catch up with him.

They passed through a dining area connected to a kitchen that would have done any chef proud. Vanessa asked Taye if he could cook. He gave her a mischievous look and said, "Sometimes."

On the edge of the west wing, he showed her a cozy room that smelled of turpentine, oil and acrylic paint. On the sink at the center of the room, brushes soaked in clear liquid, and a stack of half-finished canvases lined the back wall. She lifted the cover on the canvas in front of the only two chairs in the room.

The woman in the portrait lounged on black velvet in a sheer black, barely there gown that left little of her slim but curvaceous form to the imagination. Gold-streaked hair spilled outward. Vanessa took in a quick breath. *She* was the woman. The pose and the gown had been published in the Sweetheart Dreams Catalog. She turned away from the portrait.

Words flowed from Taye like a warm waterfall. "I'll never forget how it was when you started with Sweetheart Dreams. You were my golden dream girl, the perfect woman. I promised myself that one day I would get to know you and prove that you were real."

A strong emotion gripped her and for the life of her, she couldn't identify it. Excitement? Anticipation?

Vanessa realized that she needed a moment to regroup and focus her attention on her assignment. Taye Rollins was an attractive man, but not the first she'd encountered. She had been so sidelined by his attentions and the emotions he inspired that she hadn't learned anything to help with the assignment.

"Where is the ladies' room?" she asked. "I need a minute."

Taye led her through a hall of closed doors and around a bend to a flower-filled bath off one of the bedrooms. Once he was certain she knew how to get back to his painting room, he promised to wait there.

In the bathroom, she combed her hair and smoothed her outfit. Dampening a cloth with cold water, she patted her face and neck until she felt refreshed. Then she sat on the flower-patterned sofa with a fresh-cut rose from the vase and gave herself a talking to.

A thorn cut into the flesh of one finger and she pulled it out to absently rub the spot. Getting in with Taye on a friendly basis was good for the assignment, but getting in deep would make things worse. She was here on business, not pleasure, she reminded herself.

She suspected that he wouldn't wait long before coming to check on her. Her look around would have to be quick. She slipped out of her heels and cracked open the bathroom door. The hallway outside was empty.

Vanessa headed out, then stopped short and ducked into an alcove when she realized that people were coming her way. Her heart thundered in her chest.

A man's voice boomed loud and angry over Taye's singing on the stereo system. She recognized Jerrell Vaughn's voice, but gone was the smooth, cool, vaguely amused tone he'd used all evening. His tone now was rough with fury.

"Bitch! Did you think I wouldn't find out?"

"J-Jerrell, I d-didn't know it would turn out like that!" The woman's voice wavered with fear. "You know I wouldn't do anything to jeopardize your business!"

"I don't know a damn thing!" he roared.

From the alcove, Vanessa peeked around the corner, wondering if she should show herself. She was just in time to see the impeccably dressed Jerrell open a door and grab a tall, slim, blonde in a gold dress by the arm. The woman hadn't been in the limousine with them, but Vanessa recognized her from the apartment complex. She was a model named Mila.

The woman struggled with Jerrell, her green eyes filling with tears as she tried to pull away. "Please, talk to Carouthers. He promised to straighten things out!"

"Why the hell do you think we're having this talk?" Jerrell grabbed Mila by the neck and threw her into the next room.

She must have tumbled into a wall, because Vanessa heard a *thud* and the surrounding walls and doors shook with the impact. The door slammed shut.

Vanessa's heart was in her throat as she charged out from the alcove. On the other side of the closed door, she listened to Jerrell and Mila argue. She wasn't going to let him beat up or kill Mila if she could help it.

When she heard a flat, punching sound and an answering feminine cry, she put her hand on the knob and turned it. The door jerked inward, nearly throwing Vanessa off balance and into the room. With a low groan, Mila gingerly squeezed past Vanessa, her face wet with tears. The right side of her face was already starting to swell.

Vanessa was filled with anger. She wanted to kick Jerrell's ass.

"What the hell are you doing here?" he asked. "This is my private room, my private business."

"I was in the bathroom and I thought I heard somebody scream," Vanessa answered. "I came to see if I could help."

He laughed, an incredibly chilling, cackling sound that raised goose bumps on Vanessa's arms. "Did you scream, Mila?"

Mila cowered outside the door, holding one side of her face. "I—I might have cried out when I stumbled into the wall…. I've had too much to drink."

"Do you need Vanessa to help you?" he asked, his voice dripping with kindness.

Mila's eyes pleaded with Vanessa, silently asking her to go away. "No, I don't need any help."

"Do I need to show you the way out?" Jerrell asked Vanessa, an undercurrent of threat in his voice.

"Vanessa!" Taye's voice interrupted them. He had just come into the hall. "I was looking for you. What happened? Did you get lost?"

Were you snooping around? He didn't ask, but Vanessa imagined that she saw the question in his eyes. "I thought I heard somebody scream, so I came out to help," she explained.

"Is everything all right?" Taye asked, directing his attention to Jerrell and Mila.

Mila used the story about stumbling again, Vanessa was sure that no one believed her. Jerrell told Taye that he and Mila were on their way to the kitchen to get ice for her face. Both assured Taye that everything was fine.

Taye extended a hand to Vanessa. "Shall we continue the tour? I've still got a lot to show you."

Letting her fingers close on his, Vanessa nodded and allowed him to lead her away. "If you believe she fell, then I've got a bridge you can buy," Vanessa muttered as they passed his painting studio.

Taye pulled her up short. "We grew up in the same neighborhood, joined the same gang and learned a lot about life together, so Jerrell is like a brother to me," he said, "but he can be rude, crude, rough and violent. He's got his own room here and is welcome to stay, whenever he wants, but I don't watch him 24/7 or try to control him. We're adults, Vanessa. Mila went along with his program and refused our help. What do you want me to do?"

Shrugging, she met his gaze. This wasn't the time to blow it with Taye. "I guess I really wanted to help her," she confessed.

He gently caressed her face with his fingertips. "You can't save the world, Vanessa. I learned that one a long time ago. You were brave to face Jerrell in a rage. Don't do it again. I won't let him hurt you, but if I'm not there, his temper could get the best of him." Moving in, his soft lips gently caressed hers.

Threads of excitement shot through her, filling her with heat. Melting, she closed her eyes and cupped his head, her fingers sinking into his thick hair. Her body screamed for more.

He backed her to the wall and stood so close that warmth from the entire length of his body enveloped her. His mouth opened, hot and insistent on hers, his tongue stroking and dancing across her lips and tongue with a skill and passion that stole her breath. Vanessa found herself trembling.

She was flattered to note that his hands trembled, too, but he stopped short of letting them wander all over her. She gave him points for that.

"I'm living the dream," he whispered close to her ear. "Let's go to my room for some privacy. I promise something you'll never forget."

The words brought her out of her daze. She should have known he'd get around to asking. Vanessa placed the palms of her hands on his chest. Yes, she was really attracted to Taye Rollins, but she wasn't going to give in to it like the groupies he was probably used to.

He leaned back, making eye contact and looking for her answer. One finger traced the outline of her lips. "Or we could take it slow."

"I think that's a good idea."

Accepting the rejection gracefully, Taye moved away from her. "Let's hit the music studio. I'll show you some of the tracks we're working on."

Taye's executive assistant, Deborah, hovered over Cody for what seemed like hours. He wondered if she was doing her job by baby-sitting him, was hungry for masculine attention, or was simply interested in him. A nice lady with an attractive face, she was also a busty babe. Too bad he wasn't interested.

Realizing that she wasn't going away anytime soon, Mackenzie stood and followed a band member out of the room. Sticking close to him, Deborah offered him a tour of the common areas. Cody agreed. He'd seen Vanessa head off with Taye at least an hour ago. It was time to gather a little Intel of his own.

Mackenzie wasn't used to seeing such displays of wealth. As he was shown around, he realized that other than the elegant furnishings, there were few personal effects visible on the large estate. He also noted that security personnel circulated, apparently ensuring that the guests stuck to the certain areas. Taye Rollins had the entire east wing of the house for himself and his guests.

After a while, it became obvious that Deborah wasn't going to show him anything that might give him insight into Taye Rollins or help him with the investigation. He would have to find a way to wander about on his own, or wait for Vanessa and hope she had been able to gather some information.

Cody attached himself to one of the video machines in Taye's arcade. He talked games with some of the other people there and fought a couple of Alien Warrior challenges. Deborah stayed with him for a while, then got bored and went back to the party room.

Taye's guests drifted in and out of the arcade in groups of two and three. Cody casually followed a couple around a bend and down a hall to an area where two tough-looking men with their hands in their pockets loitered outside a closed door. One sported short, skinny braids and the other had a gleaming, bald head. Cody figured they were the guards. Music, conversation and laughter from the room spilled out into the hallway. It sounded like a party.

The guards scanned the couple and nodded as they approached. They apparently knew the two guests.

"Hold up a minute, bro," the big, bald one said, catching sight of Cody following close behind them. He put a hand on the bulge of what must have been a gun in his pocket. "I haven't seen you here before."

Cody explained that he hadn't been there before, but he'd come from the concert with Taye and his crew. The couple opened the door to go in and the raucous sounds increased, the scent of marijuana drifting out into the hallway. Cody watched them go inside. He caught a glimpse of people sitting on couches inside the room. He was on to something. At the very minimum, they were smoking weed inside.

The two apparent guards eyed him suspiciously. "Did Jerrell say it was okay for you to come back here?" the bald one asked.

Cody had barely met Jerrell on the trip in the limousine on their way from the concert and he wasn't about to get caught in a lie. To put things in the best light possible, he told them that he knew Jerrell.

"What's your name?" the one with the skinny braids asked, lifting a clipboard.

Mackenzie gave his name.

The guard studied the list. "You ain't on here, man."

"That means we can't let you in," the bald one said with an almost palpable glee. "And that's really too bad, 'cause there's some good shit up in there!"

Both guards laughed.

The door opened again. This time a man in a blue business suit came out glassy eyed and sniffing hard.

"See what I mean?" the bald one said, chuckling. "Find Jerrell and talk to him. He'll set you up and put you on the list for the private party."

Private party? Cody was pretty sure the guy who'd just come out had been doing coke. It was Taye Rollins's estate, but the okay for entry into the drugstore had to come from Jerrell Vaughn? What kind of setup was this? Taye had to know this was going on in his home. Why would a man with his obvious skills and talent jeopardize everything with such an operation?

The DEA agent in him wanted to pull out the official ID and bust all of them, but he'd learned the hard way to keep his cool. He had a specific mission here, and arresting a few druggies and low-level sellers wasn't going to net the big fish running the gang.

With an understanding nod, Cody turned and went back to the arcade.

Chapter 10

Realizing that she was much too early for her meeting with Mackenzie, Vanessa jogged six laps at the track and moved from machine to machine at the gym, working off enduring frustration and the fattening food she'd eaten last night.

Vanessa had had a restless night, but she refused to dwell on it. Long ago she'd learned to never let sex rule her world or her decisions. She'd learned that lesson from the man who'd headed her first modeling agency and been her lover—until the next top model came along. Vanessa was crushed because she'd been convinced that they were in love.

Mackenzie met her at the little coffee shop down the street from the gym. Her jaw tightened with anger when she told him about the violent incident between Jerrell and Mila. She hated to see any woman cowed by a man. That's why she'd chosen her charity.

The incident had made her critical and a little wary of Taye, too, because Jerrell felt free to beat women in his friend's home. Lord knows what else he was up to. Hearing Carouthers's name had also been a surprise. Now they had to find out if it was the Carouthers who was on the DEA suspect list.

"I'm glad you didn't blow your cover," Cody remarked coolly.

Not willing to listen to even a hint of criticism, she met his gaze with a challenge in her eyes. "I know what I'm doing."

"Yeah, you do," he acknowledged. He set down his fork. "But be careful of Rollins. He seemed real taken with you. You had him drooling. I didn't see him talk to anyone else all evening."

"I could say the same about you and that executive assistant."

"Yeah." Cody grinned. "But I wasn't interested." He paused. "You really like Rollins, don't you?"

Asked point-blank, what could she do but tell the truth? "Yes," she admitted, determined not to elaborate. Her face felt hot. Was she actually blushing after all these years?

She glanced up from her fruit bowl to find him scanning her face intently.

"Be careful," he repeated. "It almost looked as if he'd hooked *you*. You drop your guard and you could blow your cover. We're dealing with dangerous people, remember? I'm not messing up my record of successful operations and I'm not jeopardizing my life just because you want to jump his bones."

She glared at him. "You're going too far with this, Mackenzie." Vanessa snapped. "I'm just doing my job and I've got my priorities straight, so quit trying to run my life."

Mackenzie leveled a stare that she met angrily. The silence fairly crackled with the intensity of their disagreement. Neither backed down as it lengthened. Finally, Mackenzie shrugged and began his summary of his visit to the arcade and discovery of the guarded private party room. There had been drugs there, marijuana at a minimum, and probably cocaine and more.

As she sipped black coffee laced with artificial sugar she felt uneasy. Details were missing, but no way could she discount the connection among Taye, Jerrell and Carouthers. They were probably members of the gang she and Mackenzie were trying to identify.

"I didn't actually see the guns, but the two guards kept putting their hands in their pockets and there was something bulky in each of them."

Vanessa swallowed against a dry mouth. She knew that appearances could be deceiving, but things looked really bad. Could she be so deeply attracted to a man who'd had a hand in the murders of two models? No matter how she felt, she would do her job by getting the evidence needed to ensure an arrest and conviction.

She and Mackenzie agreed that Taye, Jerrell and Carouthers were the ones to focus on.

As the weekend approached, Taye called and invited Vanessa to lunch on his boat. Knowing how busy he was, she was surprised and flattered. It was an opportunity she couldn't afford to miss, and besides, she wanted to see him. Because she would be working, she tried to suppress the anticipation running through her. No matter what Taye thought, this was not a date.

Heat curled up from the sand and blacktop, but the breathtaking blue of the Atlantic Ocean mesmerized Vanessa as she drove along the beach. Sunlight sparkled off the water like diamonds. Seagulls flew overhead and fished the water.

She arrived at the marina in a vintage halter shorts suit with Jimmy Choo metallic leather Pilar sandals. Taye met her at the entrance and stared long and hard.

"You look good."

"You do, too," she murmured, taking in his Taye-Wear white Egyptian-cotton shirt with blue "T" accents, matching slacks and white captain's hat with his name embroidered in gold across the navy brim.

Taking her hand he slowly leaned forward and kissed her cheek. As she inhaled the fresh, exotic scent of his cologne, her imagination wreaked havoc on her common sense.

He led her to a big white yacht moored in the third slip and helped her on board. The boat's name, *The Getaway*, was printed along the side. A smooth-lined, white curving concoction of fiberglass, stainless steel and tinted windows, the boat was gorgeous. It was a SeaRay SunSport 705, just like the one her friend Clayton's father had just purchased. It was a big and luxurious yacht. Glancing around, Vanessa decided that a cruise down to the Bahamas would be a breeze. There were two bedrooms, a large living room and a bathroom. Following Taye to the cockpit, she quickly discovered that there was no crew on board. It would be the first time she'd actually been alone with him.

"You know how to drive?" she asked.

"I make it a point to know how to operate everything I own," he replied. "When I have a lot of guests, I use a captain, but for lunch, I wanted just the two of us. Do you know anything about boating?"

She told him that she'd taken a United States Power Squadron's public boating class in New York and an old boyfriend had taught her how to pilot. Without a lot of fanfare, he untied the boat and they took off.

With her sunglasses perched on her nose, Vanessa sat beside Taye and relaxed while he maneuvered the boat through the water. Tinted windows filtered the afternoon sunlight and cooling air swirled around them.

"Sometimes I just want to board this baby and keep going until I run out of money or water," he confided.

"Sometimes I feel like that, too," she admitted. "What would you be escaping from?"

He stared out at the horizon. "If you haven't figured it out, I'm a workaholic. When I'm on a roll, there's almost nothing I can't do but in spite of all my success, my biggest mistakes still live on to trip me up and hold me back."

That sounded painful. Vanessa studied him, sensing frustration. "And which mistakes are those?" she prodded softly.

His expression briefly turned defiant, then his lips curved upward and he surprised her with a mysterious-sounding chuckle. "A secret for a secret, Vanessa. I give up one of mine and you have to give up one of yours. Whatever it is, it stays between us. Deal?"

She couldn't think of a better way to learn Taye's secrets. "Deal," she echoed, ignoring a cautioning inner voice.

"Belonging to a gang was one of my biggest mistakes," he said. "I stole stuff and I hurt people and we sold drugs. My big excuse is that my mom had died and Pops was too deep into the bottle to know or care about me. The Street Killers took me in and became my family, and like family, there's always a connection. I quit the gang before I turned eighteen, but the gang didn't quit me. I was already starting to make a name for myself, even then."

"By the gang, you mean Jerrell and some of the groups you develop and sponsor?"

He nodded. "They have talent, but the real deal is not as rosy as it seems. There's always a threatening new problem that I have to resolve before it destroys the things I've worked for. I don't mind giving back and helping other people get to where I am, but some don't want to change or do anything hard to get what they want. The easy ways always seem to lead to trouble."

Turning her face and pretending interest in a tiny little island that was barely more than a patch of grass, Vanessa gripped her chair. Taye had just as good as told her that he couldn't control his crew. She could understand that since they were all grown men, but couldn't he just kick them off his property? Stop associating with them?

"Okay, your turn," he announced.

She crossed her fingers beneath her side of the console, hoping she wouldn't have to lie. "What do you want to know?"

"Why did you stop modeling at the top of your game? Your career was off the hook."

Searching for a plausible answer, she wet her lips.

"I gave *you* the truth," he muttered just under his breath.

Vanessa couldn't believe she was that transparent. She'd barely considered lying. She'd never told anyone about that chapter in her past and she'd done her best to bury it. Somehow it kept coming back to bite her, just as Taye had said. "Ask a different question."

"C'mon, Vanessa," he said, "it's what I want to know."

Vanessa hated lies, so the various other excuses that came to mind wouldn't pass her lips. She suddenly realized that other than in the therapy sessions at the private clinic where she'd had her recovery, she'd never admitted to having been an addict. Tears pricked her eyelids. "I was addicted to cocaine." The words had come out in a rush. She couldn't quite believe she'd said them.

He shut off the engine to pull her into his arms.

"N-no one knows," she added, surprised that the tears were really flowing now.

"I'll never tell," he said, massaging her back and letting his lips brush her temple.

Inside she cringed. She would have to tell Mackenzie everything Taye had said.

"Are you more upset by the fact that you did it or by the fact that you couldn't stop?"

"That I couldn't stop," she admitted. She felt the heat of his mouth close to her ear.

"That's what I thought. I didn't want to make you cry. I just want you to trust me. Can you do that?"

She nodded, realizing that whether it made sense or not, it was the truth. "Do you trust *me?*" she asked.

"With my life, baby," he answered. "I'm a man who goes with his instincts."

For a moment she couldn't breathe. He didn't know how much his life was in her hands.

Taye burst into laughter. "If you could see the expression on your face!"

Vanessa forced natural-sounding laughter from her lips.

"You insist on taking it slow, but we both know there's something real between us," he said confidently.

"I'm not sure what this is between us," she said as he let her go. He checked his chart against the landscape.

"Yeah, but it's too strong to walk away from, isn't it?"

She nodded.

He set the chart down and pulled her close again.

The heat and strength of his body gave a whole new meaning to the word *comfort*. Her one hand gripped his biceps and the other burrowed into the thick hair at his nape. Their mouths fused, and his tongue explored hers with such skill and passion that she slumped back in her chair and tingled all the way down to her toes.

Naked desire shone in his eyes. "Say the word, Vanessa. It's going to be real good for both of us."

Her body was still humming like a well oiled machine. It didn't take much imagination to know that what he said was true. Still, her determination to finish the assignment before she gave in to her need for Taye was strong.

She could only look at him.

He took her mouth in another dazzling kiss. "Your loss," he murmured as he restarted the engines and headed farther out. Twenty minutes later he dropped anchor close to a lush little island filled with tall green grass, exotic-looking trees and fragrant red flowers.

On deck beneath an overhanging tree, he served a gourmet lunch. Afterward, they sipped Riesling and lazed side by side in two chaise lounge chairs on the rear deck.

"I was hoping you'd star in one of the videos for my new CD," he said as they discussed the fact that her Miami photo shoot was nearly done. "I've always wanted you in one of my videos—and the pay is good."

Vanessa guessed that the fact she'd been telling the other models that she needed money had reached him. She'd already told Taye that her parents refused to support her as long as she was modeling.

Posing as a woman in need of money, she could hardly turn down his offer. But the truth was, she didn't have to think twice. She *wanted* to be in his video—as long as he didn't make it degrading to her and other women—because she liked his music and welcomed the exposure.

Lifting an eyebrow and bracing for a fight, she said, "I'd like to be in your video, but I'm not putting on a thong and turning my back on the camera to shake my ass."

Taye chuckled. "Let's face it, sex sells. You know that as well as I do. I'm not asking you to do that on camera," he said suggestively, "but I'm ready to cheer you on, anytime the urge hits you."

"Don't hold your breath," Vanessa quipped.

"You might surprise yourself."

"Only if *you're* ready to put on a thong and dance on *my* table," she put in.

"Deal." He extended a hand so she could shake it. Then he laughed.

"You're incorrigible!" Vanessa gave him a playful push. "Could *anyone* make you do something you didn't want to?"

Taye's face turned serious. "We've shared enough secrets for today, Vanessa," he said. "We should be getting back."

Somehow her question had destroyed the mood. Taye was obviously dealing with some serious issues. Vanessa watched in silence as he pulled anchor and headed back, the waning light drawing harsh shadows on his face. She hoped his secrets did not include drugs…or murder.

Vanessa spent much of the next week at Taye's estate working out her scenes in his video and trying to get everything right. He wanted to stick close to home, where he could work other projects at the same time, so they used a set built on his property specifically for the video. While there, she used every opportunity to familiarize herself with his mansion and its occupants.

The outfit Taye wanted her to wear became a big problem. It was little more than a skimpy bunch of beads hanging off her shoulders and breasts. Not only was it too revealing, it wasn't classy or flattering to her figure. When talks with the wardrobe person yielded nothing, Vanessa went to Taye.

He was dividing his time between the video and a new group he had in the studio. When she slipped into the room, they were working hard on a new song. She waited twenty minutes before he left the group.

Taye led Vanessa outside onto a veranda to talk. He remained silent as she raged on about the costume, but his eyes had turned dark and brooding. When she finished, he told her that he had designed the costume just for her. He looked angry, but it was too late to take back some of the things she'd said. Somehow, Vanessa couldn't bring herself to apologize.

"So what do we do now?" she asked. "I'm not wearing that. Do you have a different outfit for me, or were you thinking of getting someone else?"

"I did make a list of other models, you know," he said testily.

"Then you should use one of them," she declared. "Maybe she'll even be happy to wear that outfit outside of your bedroom, too."

In the ensuing silence, Vanessa counted to five. When Taye said nothing further, she headed for the house.

"You're throwing a hissy fit over nothing," he called after her.

"Am I?" She strode back to get in his face. "I have my image and reputation to consider. Modeling is a business. Remember? Contrary to common belief, I can turn down an assignment and find another. You can pay me for the days I've worked so far."

Vanessa went to get her things. She was sorry to be leaving on such short notice for a number of reasons. She liked Taye and his music. Then there was the fact that so far, she'd only been able to check out a few of the rooms. She'd also promised to get Mackenzie in to check the area he'd seen after the concert. Vanessa bit her lip. *I'll find another way to come back,* she promised herself. *I can always come back to visit.*

Taye was standing near the front entrance when she headed for her car. He waved the folded sheets of paper in his hand. "This is business. Vanessa, you signed a contract."

They stared at one another. "Give me something I can work with," she said.

Shifting his feet, he massaged a spot on the back of his neck. "Give me a couple of days. I'll see what I can do."

Vanessa went home hoping the new outfit would be something less than X-rated. If not, she was going to have to work on another sure-fire way back into Taye's mansion.

Vanessa didn't tell Mackenzie that she'd stopped work on the video. She didn't want to hear him complain. She came up with a list of reasons to go back to Taye's and discovered it was pitifully short.

Two days later, she got a package in the mail. Once she saw it was from Taye, she ripped it open. Inside she found a stunning, sheer metallic-gold dress with smooth, sleek lines that draped her body and emphasized every curve. With a sigh of relief, she called Taye to restart work on the video.

Vanessa was amazed to discover the sheer volume of takes it took to produce the effect Taye wanted. Between takes and while the camera crew shot Taye and the band, she roamed the house freely. By staying away from the guards, she'd managed to search a good portion of the house. When Mackenzie came down to "watch the taping" and do a little surveillance, she distracted the guards while he searched the room that had been used for the private parties. It had been secured, but Mackenzie worked the lock like a pro. Later, he told Vanessa that inside he'd discovered a converted closet with an expensive lock. Inside was an area that served as a sort of pharmacy. It was filled with pills, marijuana and coke. He had more than enough to pull a raid right then, but they were after the people running the organization.

Mackenzie's discovery forced Vanessa to focus more effort on the job. She couldn't even look at Taye without something tensing deep inside.

On the video set, Vanessa watched Taye perform his part of the scene. Pretending to have a headache, she put on a robe, retrieved the gun from her purse, and accepted Taye's offer to lie down in a guest bedroom. But instead, she slipped past the guards to find her way to Taye's room. He'd left it out of her private tour, but she'd discovered the location through the process of elimination.

His room was clearly that of a man who liked to play. A large bay window and beautiful French doors showcased a glorious view of the drifting sailboats on mirrored water. Sunlight drenched the room. Central to the room was a large, custom-made bed of wood and leather, with circular metal accents that left no doubt that the owner was a man.

She crossed a blue carpet with a design motif resembling waves and focused on his desk. She didn't know what she was looking for, but she figured that if Taye was involved in the drug business, there would be records on his personal computer.

The computer was protected with the latest antivirus software and a password system that would lock out intruders after three failed login attempts. She settled back into his soft leather captain's chair, knowing that she would have only two chances at his password.

Her fingers smoothed the butter-soft leather and curled around the arm of the chair. What would Taye Rollins use for a password?

Closing her eyes, she let her mind wander. She thought about the man, his art, his music, the clothing line… Music was at the center of a lot of his actions, but his password choice would involve some other aspect of his life.

Vanessa began typing in the registration numbers she'd seen stamped on the hull of his boat, *The Getaway*. Asterisks filled the space next to the blinking cursor. Holding her breath, she pressed enter. *Yeah!* She was in.

Vanessa did a quick and efficient search of his computer. She found poetry and music and programs used to design clothing, but no bank transfers or account information. She'd all but given up when she found a song titled "Street."

The words to the song were so filled with gibberish and typographical errors that they made no sense. Studying them closely, it became clear that she wasn't looking at typos. It was a code hidden in a song. She pressed the button on Taye's printer and made a copy.

Folding the paper into a small packet, she slipped it into her pocket. Then she closed the file.

Vanessa jumped at the click of someone turning the doorknob. The cool feel of the nine-millimeter pistol in her pocket reassured her.

She heard voices. Someone was still at the door. Turning down the speaker sound, she quickly selected "shutdown" on the computer menu, confirmed and then switched off the monitor. Scooting to the bed, she pulled back the covers and dived in.

Chapter 11

When the door opened, Vanessa lay stretched out on the bed, the covers at her waist. She opened her eyes slowly, feigning something close to sleep. Jerrell stood there with one of the guards.

Jerrell glanced around the room, a suspicious look on his face. "What are you doing in here?"

"What does it look like?" she asked in a challenging tone.

He dismissed the guard. "Uh, I don't know. Did you hear somebody scream?"

He was obviously referring to the visit where she'd caught him manhandling Mila. Vanessa yawned and stretched her arms above her head, hoping he'd get the hint. "Not yet."

He laughed.

She managed a smile despite the tension stiffening her back. Jerrell was like a poisonous snake, capable of striking any second. She was wary of him.

"So Taye knows you're in here?" he asked, glancing around the room and then back to the bed to scan her body inch by inch.

She fought the urge to cover the skin left bare by the plunging neckline of her robe. Her skin crawled beneath his inspection.

"He should be along any minute now," she said, pulling the covers up. Her statement was true, except that Taye would be checking on her in the guest room.

"Okay." He executed a quick turn as if to close the door and leave, then turned back to face her. "By the way, I heard you were looking for ways to make some extra cash."

She propped her head on the palm of one hand. "It's true."

He assessed her with his eyes. "Well I've got a proposal for you, if you can be discreet."

"What do you want me to do?" she asked.

He hesitated. "You seem okay, but if you do this job for me, you'll have to behave yourself."

"What do you mean?" Vanessa allowed her tone to harden. *The dirty dog.* How could Jerrell Vaughn talk to anyone about behaving themselves?

He braced a palm against the door frame. "There were rumors about you and some cokeheads a couple of years ago. Whether it's true or not is not my business...."

Vanessa gritted her teeth, almost certain Taye had kept her confidence about her past. She was going to enjoy seeing the cops cart Jerrell off to jail. "What do you want me to do?"

He shrugged. "You'll have to do as you're told, but it won't be difficult. This isn't the time or place to go into detail. We'll talk about it over lunch tomorrow. Meet me at Malone's, eleven-thirty."

Her eyes narrowed. Why was he meeting her away from the house? And why couldn't they talk about it now? She hoped it was because Taye was not involved in whatever Jerrell was up to.

"Will Taye be there?" she asked.

"No, this is between you and me." He checked the empty hall behind him.

She realized that Jerrell could be setting her up for any number of things, but she would have bet her gun that he wanted her to move drugs for him.

He lowered his voice. "Just so you know, I know of some other models who ended their...careers early because they got cocky and tried to steal from me."

Her breath caught in her throat. She was pretty sure he was talking about Gena and Bianca. Her eyes widened as she realized that her shaking fingers were actually stroking the gun beneath the covers.

Angry as hell, she saw herself fitting the smooth metal into the palm of her hand, lifting the barrel and aiming with precision to hit Jerrell Vaughn right between the eyes. It was the least she could do for Gena and Bianca.

"Are you threatening me?" she managed to say in a voice that shook for reasons very different from what Jerrell probably assumed.

He actually grinned, looking for all the world as if he were harmless.

Dropping his hand, he shifted his feet and his expression turned serious. "No, I'm not threatening you. Just making sure you know the limits, Vanessa. I don't play when it comes to business and my partners don't, either. See you tomorrow."

He shut the door in her face.

Frozen in her spot on the bed, she drew in a shaky breath. With a sigh of relief, she removed her hand from the gun. She couldn't shoot Jerrell, no matter how much he deserved it. A better move was to gather all the evidence and let the cops cart him off to prison.

For several moments she lay back against the pillows, letting herself recover from the confrontation. Then tossing back the covers, she got up and began to straighten the bed. Better to find Taye on the set before he found her in his room.

But before she could make it to the area where they were shooting the video, Taye caught up with her in the kitchen. His gaze was more intense than usual.

"Feeling better?" he asked.

He'd been searching for something in her face. "I was just coming back to finish my part of today's shooting," she said as she accepted his extended hand.

Vanessa had noticed that he seemed to find ways to touch her all the time. Now he drew her close for a hug, his fingers tangling in her hair. "What did you do to get Jerrell so pumped?" he murmured close to her ear. "He's talking kind of crazy and I haven't seen him doing any drugs."

Tilting her head away from his she widened her smile. "I didn't go to the guest room, I went to your room instead. I actually used your bed. Jerrell found me in there."

He was silent for a couple of beats.

Fighting guilt, she maintained eye contact. His gaze bored right through her.

She didn't know whether he was suspicious that she'd searched his room or worried that she'd taken something. Then it hit her. He was jealous that Jerrell had discovered her there. Taye Rollins was pouting.

"You're not jealous, are you? We could always go back to your room for a while," she offered. The fact that she'd made the offer surprised her. She was already worried about having gotten in too deep with Taye.

He flashed even, white teeth at her. "Did I look that pitiful?"

She waited a few moments to emphasize her point, then returned the smile. "Yeah."

Suddenly so close that a sheet of paper couldn't have fit between them, his tone turned husky. "Are you offering me a little pity sex?"

Her hair brushed his cheek as she lifted her head. "No, but we could nap together."

"How about a lot of pity sex?"

"No, but we could nap together," she repeated.

"That's not enough to satisfy a man."

"I'm not trying to satisfy *a* man."

"Then how about a little satisfaction for *this* man?"

She trailed a finger all the way from the opening in his shirt to the tightness in his crotch. "You are desirable, Taye. Believe me. But I've learned a lot about the world and myself, and I'm not in the satisfaction business for anyone but myself, at least for right now."

"Okay, Vanessa." He traced her lips with a fingertip and tapped her chin. "But the next time you're in my bed, I have to be there, too. Deal?"

"Deal." She felt the corners of her mouth turn up.

Taye wasn't smiling. "I like you, Vanessa. There's something about you that I don't want to let go and it ain't just because you're beautiful. I've had beautiful women before. *I want you.* Sometimes I think I'm halfway in love with you." His voice turned rough. "Say the word and I'm yours. Exclusively. But until then, I'm an uncommitted man with needs and desires that you've chosen not to fulfill. No pressure, but celibacy is out."

Vanessa nodded. He was being fair and honest with her, but the words hit like a slap in the face. Logically she appreciated it, but she was already discovering that logic didn't enter into her feelings when it came to Taye Rollins. She didn't know what she'd expected him to say, but this was not it.

Taye was watching her, one warm hand still at

her waist and burning through the thin material of her robe. "Does that change anything?"

Vanessa was surprised at her reaction to Taye's words. She shouldn't care who he carried on with or mind that it wouldn't be her. *But she did.*

She thought of all the boyfriend mistakes she'd made in her life and decided that this was probably a doozy. She'd risked her friendship with Clayton Mercer and had discovered that while she loved Clayton, she wasn't in love with him.

Her affair at seventeen with Anthony Volinelli, the head of the modeling agency, had shown her that just because someone took care of you, said they loved you and acted like it, didn't mean they really did. She was quickly dropped when the next rising star of a model came along. So how had Taye, whom she'd known less than a month, engaged her emotions so fully?

"My boyfriends always thought I was worth the wait," she said, regretting the words even as she spoke them.

"Oh, I know you're worth the wait," he assured her. "But I won't wait quietly, and I won't do it alone. So when you see me with someone else, know that it could have been you."

Vanessa had had enough of this conversation. She recognized a power play when she saw it. "Whatever it takes."

* * *

Using the time after an early morning run to discuss the assignment, Vanessa and Mackenzie ended up at her condo.

He was sprawled on Vanessa's couch with a bottle of water. She sat across from him, perched on the chair with a bottle of lemon water.

He stared at the paper she'd printed from Taye's computer. "It is a code," he confirmed, "but I've never seen anything quite like it. We'll let the experts take a look."

"I just hope it leads to something," she said. "I feel like I've been running in place. There's a good chance that Annika is one of their models, but I have yet to see her at Taye's. Then I found that Caribbean Mama spice jar like the one in Gena's place, but it proved to be just spice."

Cody drew a long sip from the bottle. "She could still be working for the drug gang. Maybe she's just cautious…or lucky."

Vanessa shrugged. "I get a weird vibe from her anyway. She's connected to Guerra, his design house, and she grew up in the same neighborhood as Guerra. You know, he would have been perfect. Those big shipping containers, and his relationships with the models. And then the fact that he knew Annika, too, fit the profile."

"Don't be so hard on us," Mackenzie said, placing the paper on her coffee table. "We've got evidence of a drug business through Taye Rollins and Jerrell Vaughn and there's a connection to the models. You overheard part of a conversation that indicates a connection to Carouthers. But let's talk about your lunch with Jerrell. We need to get you fitted with a wire, so that we can record everything. We'll have agents watching you in case you run into a problem."

Vanessa relived yesterday's conversation with Jerrell and grimaced. She already knew he was dangerous. "I'm betting that he had something to do with Gena's and Bianca's murders."

Cody eyed her critically. "For all we know, the models he referred to could have been just beaten or threatened—who knows?"

She did, with a gut instinct that had shown her where to focus her attention in past assignments, but arguing the point with Mackenzie was not going to help the situation.

"What's going on with you and Taye Rollins?" Mackenzie asked suddenly, breaking in on her thoughts.

She was startled and sure he'd caught a momentary flash of guilt on her face. "What do you mean?"

Cody studied her but kept his tone light. "You

two seem real close. The man is touching you every chance he gets. I've seen you kiss him."

Lifting both brows, she asked, "Is kissing against the rules?"

"No, but falling for him is. It ruins your objectivity and jeopardizes the assignment. You could be manipulated."

"He's being manipulated," she put in.

Cody set the empty water bottle on the floor. "And that bothers you, doesn't it."

"A little, because I don't like manipulating anyone."

"Vanessa, Taye's not being honest with you. He and Jerrell are running a drug business out of his house. We have enough to arrest them. We just need enough to gauge the full extent of the business and who's at the top, and make it stick. We need to meet the goals of this assignment. If Taye Rollins is involved in all of this, he's going to prison."

"Yes, I know." She folded her hands in her lap. "Don't you even wonder why a man who makes millions with his record company, his own performances and his clothing line would need to bother with drugs?"

"Huh!" Cody lifted a foot toward the coffee table, then seemed to think better of it. "Greed motivates a lot of people. Maybe he wants to be a billionaire."

Taye wasn't obsessed with money. Vanessa had seen that. She'd never seen him take drugs, either. She thought of what he'd said about quitting the gang but the gang not quitting him. Could that explain what he obviously allowed to go on in his home?

Mackenzie was studying her again, as if he could see clear through to her thoughts and didn't like what was there. "If we weren't so far along in this, I'd ask to have you replaced."

"Why? I'm doing a good job. It's because of me that we have the leads with Jerrell and Taye. Are you questioning my loyalty?"

"Not yet, but I'm concerned."

"Then get over it," she insisted angrily. "I know which side I'm on." Her voice rang with conviction. "I want to make sure that whoever is responsible for Gena's and Bianca's deaths pays for it, and I want to put this drug gang out of business."

Mackenzie waited while Vanessa showered and changed. Then he accompanied her down to the DEA's Miami Field Office to be fitted with her recording device. Since she'd called Alan late last night to tell him that she planned to use the false fingernails with the electronic bugs for her meeting with Jerrell, she was surprised to find that he'd already overnight shipped another alternative to the Miami Field Division to be examined.

Vanessa followed a female agent, Erin, into the ladies' room to have the device applied and checked out. She laughed out loud at the sight of the delicate gold belly ring, shaped like a flower. A red ruby sparkled from the center. Behind it was a tiny microphone and recorder.

She had donned a long Cavalli leopard-print skirt in caramel and cocoa rayon that rode provocatively low on her hips. The short, matching sleeveless top hung loosely above an exposed band of flesh. When she walked, the belly ring would be visible.

Erin produced a small flesh-colored device that the DEA would use to communicate with her while she was in the restaurant. It fit in her ear canal and was undetectable.

To test the setup, Vanessa and Erin discussed the Guerra fashion event while Vanessa fixed her hair. From the next room, Mackenzie added silly comments about the models, the clothes and the hats on the device in her ear. Afterward, they played back the conversation in the next room. The communicator had worked perfectly.

The thought of several agents listening to her conversation with Jerrell and waiting to pounce was unnerving. If he smelled a setup, she would have a vicious fight on her hands.

"Are you going to arrest Jerrell?" Vanessa asked, after Erin had reapplied the belly-button ring.

"It depends on what he says," Erin replied. "If he leads us to believe there is someone above him, then we'll hold off. We're not trying to take over your assignment. We're only there to help and provide a layer of protection in case things get ugly. Vanessa, you need to be very careful. From all accounts, Jerrell Vaughn is a dangerous man."

Vanessa wasn't looking forward to lunch with Jerrell. She couldn't stand him. Instinct told her that he had committed those murders.

As Vanessa made her way to Malone's, she readied herself mentally. She could take Jerrell, couldn't she? Flashes of the pictures she'd seen of the girls' bodies and apartments were making her crazy. She reminded herself that with a number of other DEA agents in the room listening, things couldn't go wrong. But she'd seen too many movies where the agent wearing the wire got killed....

Chapter 12

Vanessa entered the restaurant and went from warm, bright sunlight into the cool, dimly lit interior. Upbeat music from the eighties was playing in the background. For several moments, she could barely see. Then her eyes adjusted and she noticed a dark-haired hostess in a white blouse and long black skirt step forward.

"Vanessa Dawson?"

"Yes," Vanessa answered. She wanted to check her watch—she had thought she was early.

"Please follow me. Your party is in the private room in the back."

Vanessa followed the hostess across the hardwood floor. She saw a few couples eating or talking in booths, with individuals sitting alone at various spots around the room. Careful not to stare, she quickly scanned the room, wondering which of the patrons belonged to her backup team.

In the back of the restaurant, past the carved oak and leather bar, there was a banquet room. Two long rectangular tables with chairs dominated the space. In a sand-colored suit, Jerrell sat, almost hidden, at one of the booths lining each wall.

"Vanessa, glad you could make it," he said, looking up from his menu. He met her glance briefly. Then his gaze slipped to the expanse of skin below her neck.

If it hadn't been for the dimness of the lighting, she'd have sworn her dress hid nothing from him. He wasn't behaving the way you'd expect Taye's friend to act, but then, she didn't think Jerrell was anybody's friend. She returned his greeting and slipped into the other side of the booth.

Erin's voice sounded in the tiny receiver in her ear. "Vanessa, we're here if you need us. Since he'd booked the banquet room, we couldn't get seats back there, but you're coming in loud and clear. Clear your throat if you hear me."

Vanessa cleared her throat. The weird thing was that Jerrell did the same thing.

"Drink?" Jerrell asked, lifting a squat glass filled with amber liquid.

"Glass of white wine," she answered, knowing it was her least favorite. She wouldn't be tempted to drink it all.

"The food here is good, too," he said, handing her one of the menus. "I like the New York strip steak and the marinated chicken."

With all the inherent danger in the meeting, she didn't think she could eat. The truth was, she couldn't wait to get it over with, but common sense told her that Jerrell might get suspicious or fail to relax his guard if she tried to rush things.

"I'll have a salad," she murmured. Jerrell wouldn't be surprised—he was used to being around models with their weight-watching.

When the server arrived, Jerrell put in both their orders. Once they had their drinks, he gave Vanessa his full attention. "So you need to make some extra money?"

Vanessa nodded. "Yes."

He gave her a skeptical look. "I thought Taye said you came from one of those families with a lot of money."

"That doesn't mean they choose to share the money with me," she quipped, "especially if they don't like what I'm doing."

His index finger pointed to her and bobbed up and down. "Hey, I'm feeling you there. You know I've got to check you for a wire, right?"

"What do you mean?" she asked, playing dumb. The last thing she needed was him groping her. Maybe Jerrell would recognize the tiny recorder on the belly-button ring. There was a bulge in the pocket of his suit jacket and she guessed it was a gun.

Vanessa thought ahead to what she might do if Jerrell found the recorder. She wasn't sure if she could take him before he drew the gun.

He was obviously enjoying her discomfort. His eyes sparkled as he said, "C'mon, you watch television. I'll just pat you down to make sure. If you were a guy I'd make you strip. Hey, I kind of like that idea!"

Vanessa cut him short. "It's not happening." She ignored the advice Erin spoke into her ear and decided to handle this on her own.

Jerrell sat across from her, laughing hard. "I had you for a minute there."

Though not finding it the least bit funny, Vanessa pasted a small smile on her lips.

"Just stand up for a minute," he urged. "It won't take a minute."

Sensing no way out of this dilemma, she stood

reluctantly. The thought of Jerrell putting his hands on her turned her stomach and made her mad. It actually overruled her fear of him finding the recorder.

Holding out her arms, she endured his big hands patting her breasts and back, her waist and stomach. He paused when his fingers touched the belly-button ring.

"I always thought you were freaky. What's this?"

She gritted her teeth. "What does it *look* like."

He sucked in a breath. "Can I see it?"

"I'm not pulling it out for you," she snapped. "Get this over with."

He patted down her hips and buttocks, clearly enjoying it much too much, and then moved on to the outsides of her legs.

He moaned low in his throat. "You're gonna have me dreaming about this."

She rolled her eyes, her hands forming fists. Jerrell was a stupid jerk.

Having reached her ankles, he started up the insides of her legs. When he got to her knees, Vanessa moved away. "That's enough. Now you *know* I'm not wearing a wire."

Head bobbing up and down, he sat down laughing. "Yeah, I do, and I know that all that stuff you're strutting is the real thing, too."

Her ears almost whistled as the steam came out.

Suddenly she was leaning across the table, in his face. "I am not on the menu. You didn't get me here just to feel me up."

"No." He turned serious. "I need someone to do a job, you need money, and the way Taye feels about you makes it that much more rewarding."

He fell silent as the server brought their food.

"What's the job?" she asked as soon as they were alone again.

Jerrell set about cutting his steak. "I need you to pick up some packages for me in the Bahamas."

"What kind of packages?" she asked, pushing for information. "And what's inside?"

"Nothing you need to worry about, except that it's expensive and illegal. That's why I'm gonna pay you a lot of money. You don't open them and you don't do anything to cause yourself to get caught with them."

"It's drugs, isn't it?" she asked, trying to coax it out of him.

He released a sigh of annoyance. "Did I mention that I *hate* people who ask a lot of questions? It makes me suspicious. So far my instincts have been good, too. I ain't planning on going to jail. You need the money, agree to the job. Period. I promise that it's nothing explosive or terrorist related."

"If it's drugs, I could go to jail for a long time," she said.

"I'm not saying what it is you'll be transporting." He grabbed his drink. "Think of yourself as a courier."

Vanessa studied him. "What else could it be?"

"What if it *is* drugs?" Jerrell snapped. "If you do like we tell you, you won't have to worry about it. Very few of our people have been caught because we have a good system and models seldom go through the customs scrutiny others do. Still in?"

Vanessa hesitated. Erin was in her ear, demanding that she accept Jerrell's offer. With a show of resignation, she did.

He nodded. "Good. In return you'll get thirty thousand."

"Sixty," Vanessa insisted, guessing the job was worth at least that.

"Forty-five." His head dipped in acknowledgement. "I need it done within the next three weeks. You'll be going by boat and partying all the way. We'll pair you with someone who knows the ropes. I'll give you the details then."

"Is Taye a part of this? Will I be working for him, too?" She all but blurted the words out.

"No, you're working for *me*. Do you see Taye here in this room?" He forked a juicy chunk of steak into his mouth, chewed and swallowed.

Shaking her head, Vanessa pushed her salad

around on the plate with her fork. She didn't know if she could trust Jerrell to tell her the truth, but with his statement about Taye not being involved, some of the pressure inside her eased.

After setting his fork down, he removed the napkin from his lap and used it to pat his mouth. Then he scooted around to her side of the booth to trail a finger down her arm. "I can come up with all sorts of bonuses if you find a way to be nice to me."

Vanessa was about to explode. She didn't like being touched by Jerrell. She imagined her fist smashing that smooth square jaw he used to impress people who didn't really know him.

She scooted away to the edge of the booth. "I'm not interested. In case you hadn't noticed, I'm kind of seeing Taye. I thought you two were friends."

"More like family," he corrected. "But why should he have all the fun? You know how that is— you can fight like hell but you're still family, no matter what." His gaze was lazy as he looked at her. "There's something I don't understand about you. You're a fool to go this route to get the extra money. Taye's got a thing for you. Big time. As long as you've got his nose open like that, he'll give you anything you want."

She stood, tired of being in Jerrell's company and somehow feeling beaten. "I wouldn't use Taye like that," she declared. By now, it was obvious that the DEA agents weren't going to close in and arrest Jerrell. "Are we done?"

He waved a hand at her. "Yeah. Don't discuss this with anybody. You'll get your trip information in the mail and a phone call with the pick up time and directions to the place. When you get back, you'll get another call with the delivery information. The stuff is mine. Don't open it, don't tamper with it."

Nodding, she turned and walked out of the restaurant.

Erin's voice sounded in her ear. "Good work."

Vanessa's legs shook as she approached her car. She'd actually made it through the meeting. She drove back to her complex, checking her rear view mirror all the way. Her pulse was still racing.

Chapter 13

Vanessa was back on Miami Beach with the crew to do a few cleanup shots for the magazine. When the work was done, she hurried to change into her street clothes while the dressing room was still empty. After weeks in Miami, she'd learned to avoid some of the stress of temptation—she knew which models liked to snort coke. She nearly bumped into Savannah, who was heading out.

Savannah looked fabulous. She had an expensive hair-coloring job, a precision haircut to match and a rich tan. When Vanessa complimented her, Savannah positively glowed. Then she asked Vanessa to a party that her new boyfriend was giving. Vanessa agreed with seeming reluctance, but was secretly elated to hear that Savannah's new boyfriend was none other than Caulfield Carouthers.

"Can I bring a date?" Vanessa asked, thinking that she'd use it as an excuse to get Mackenzie in.

Savannah paused, a soulful look in her eyes. "Actually I was hoping you wouldn't. Caulfield has a friend coming from out of town to look at some property and I sort of promised to find him a date."

"I suppose I could come without a date," Vanessa reasoned aloud, "but I'm sort of seeing someone."

Savannah's laughter rang out. "Does 'sort of' seeing someone count?"

Vanessa's brows went up. "The point is that I'm not looking right now," she said.

Savannah touched her arm. "Don't worry about it. Seriously."

Vanessa smiled. "Okay, I won't. So what should I wear?"

Savannah looked downright happy to have things settled. "After-five, but not formal. Dress to impress."

Vanessa stepped into her shoes. "I will. By the way, I know Caulfield. We went to the same school and his sister Lindy was in my class."

"How fascinating," Savannah said, looking as if

Vanessa had somehow burst her bubble. "I'll tell him you're coming. I'm sure he'll be excited."

Would he? Vanessa wondered. She was getting close to solving the puzzle of Caulfield's connection to Jerrell so she was looking forward to the evening.

Hours later Vanessa donned her black Azzaro dress with the low net-covered neckline that was outlined with Swarovski crystals. She added a black pair of Manolos with gold flowers on the straps.

Outside, a warm wind whipped the air about and the ocean rose and fell like a caged animal. News reports were full of warnings about Tropical Storm Charlie coming in from the Caribbean. It was expected to hit the Miami area by morning. That gave Vanessa plenty of time to get home tonight and make a decision about going to a shelter.

With the directions Savannah had given her, Vanessa drove to Caulfield's Miami waterfront estate in the exclusive area of Palm Island. She parked in the spot indicated by a security guard. The effects of the approaching storm were more pronounced on Palm Island. Wind grabbed and whipped her hair and the ocean sprayed the shoreline as she strolled toward a white, Greco-Roman inspired masterpiece of a mansion. Tall Corinthian columns lined the covered walkway and welcomed her into the home.

A butler greeted her in the grand entry foyer and checked her name on a list. As she glanced up at the midnight-blue twenty-five-foot ceiling complete with realistically twinkling stars, Vanessa noted that the Miami estate was much more opulent than the Carouthers' estate in New York.

She reasoned that either the rumors she'd heard about financial problems plaguing the publishing family weren't true, or Carouthers was adding money to the family coffers with a little help from the drug gang. Her stilettos clicked on imported white marble as she followed the butler to the great room.

In a red Ungaro dress with spaghetti straps and a plunging neckline, Savannah stood at the marble fireplace, deep in conversation with Caulfield and an attractive brown-haired man. The man's custom-made Italian dinner jacket and matching black pants covered him in a way that screamed money and success. When he shifted to look at her, he flashed movie star teeth in genuine appreciation. Vanessa found herself staring and returning the smile. Handsome, he reminded her of a well-heeled Greg Kinnear. Nothing like a good visual to keep the evening interesting, she observed.

Noting that their guest's attention was elsewhere, Caulfield and Savannah also turned. Savannah stepped forward to welcome Vanessa and give her a hug. Caulfield was pleasant and cordial as he greeted her. Asking after her parents and her little sister, he kissed her cheek. Then he introduced her to Ryan Greene and the couple lounging at the antique bar, Eldon and Shauna Patterson.

Ryan's name sounded familiar. Puzzling over that fact, Vanessa remembered that he was a major player in a real estate firm that had donated thousands to her Golden Key Foundation last year. She told him how much the gesture was appreciated. Then, seeing his interest, she explained exactly how the money had been used to help several women in the foundation's Fresh Start Program.

When Caulfield's butler announced dinner, everyone drifted into the formal dining room. To Vanessa's surprise, Caulfield had booked a live orchestra to entertain them while they ate.

The food, prepared by Caulfield's personal chef, was fabulous.

Ryan Greene was rich, handsome and a charmer. It was an irresistible combination. She laughed a lot and enjoyed herself. He was definitely what most women would consider a hot date.

After dinner, they sat on the sofas and upholstered chairs in the great room and talked. A live jazz quartet provided soothing background music. Ryan sat so close to Vanessa that she could feel his heat. When he took her hand and started massaging her fingers, she knew where he was going with his attentiveness. The fact was that she was just becoming aware of his skill at the courting game spoke volumes.

"Where are you staying?" he asked in a low, sexy tone.

Vanessa told him about her condominium on Ocean Drive.

"I'm really into you and I think you're feeling the same. We could go there," he suggested. "We could spend more time together and get to know each other."

She squeezed his hand and released it. "I can't. I've got some studio work scheduled in the morning."

"Then tomorrow?" he asked, so suave, so seemingly sensitive.

He was the type of man her family would love and he seemed nice. She couldn't bring herself to flat-out turn him down. "Call me," she said, reaching into her bag to get him one of her cards. "I don't know when I'll be done."

She wondered if he saw through the lie. For an instant, she sensed a coldness lurking just beyond those warm brown eyes. She shivered. Had she imagined it?

Caulfield's butler, Emmett, entered the room and went to his side.

"So which properties are you looking at here in Miami," she asked Ryan, changing the subject. Vanessa fixed him with the interested facial expression she'd developed for photo shots, but her ears were busy straining to hear the conversation between Carouthers and his butler. It seemed that Carouthers had asked not to be disturbed. Apparently the call was important.

"Who is it?" Carouthers snapped, his voice low.

Vanessa heard a reply that sounded like "Vaughn." Could she really be so lucky as to have a break like that? As Carouthers excused himself and left the room, she started thinking of ways to follow.

Standing, she gathered her purse. "Excuse me, I'll be right back," she told Ryan.

At the doorway to the great room, Savannah caught up with her. "Looking for the ladies' room?"

That was the most acceptable excuse. Vanessa went with the flow. "Yes, can you tell me where it is?"

Vanessa exited the room, following directions from Savannah. Savannah's detailed directions included landmarks that would indicate that she'd gone the wrong way and ventured into Carouthers' private suite. Now Vanessa knew the way.

Worried that Savannah might decide to come after her, Vanessa hurried. She looked out for the household staff. Music from the orchestra was being piped all over the house, but she heard voices and movement behind some of the doors she passed. Fiddling with the front of her dress, she switched on the belly-button recorder.

Continuing boldly, she stuck to the knotted silk Persian rug runners that ran along the center of the marble floors. They covered the telltale tapping of her heels against the marble.

Above the entrance to Caulfield's suite, the swivel-mounted camera was still and the indicator light on the motion detector was out. Hearing the muffled sound of Caulfield's voice, she followed it until she reached a partially open door. She froze and plastered herself to the wall, knowing enough not to open the door and peer inside. She didn't know how his desk was oriented and he might be facing her.

Angry and threatening, his voice sounded again. "I'm not interested in excuses, Vaughn, and I'm not going to step in and solve the problem every time you guys stumble! I've got too much at stake. Take care of it. I want the money in my account by next week."

Vanessa's thoughts raced, envisioning all sorts of connections among Jerrell and Carouthers and the suspected drug ring. What she really wanted and needed was proof. Right now she was only capturing half of the conversation.

Caulfield fell silent again.

Slowly sliding against the wall, she carefully peered through the opening. Facing the partially open door, he was hunched over a mahogany desk in an upholstered desk chair with the telephone receiver to his ear.

Gathering herself, she stepped across the opening to the other side of the hall. She held her breath, waiting. No reaction from Carouthers.

Inching along the wall, she tried the next door. It was a bedroom, that featured floor-to-ceiling windows with a view of the windswept beach, where the trees were bending in the howling wind. The weather had grown worse since she and the other guests arrived.

The large, regal-looking bed with its metal posts reaching for the ceiling was on a pedestal below a vaulted ceiling with a skylight. The room was filled with tall, traditional-style furniture.

Focusing on the slim cordless telephone next to the bed, Vanessa entered the room. She covered the mouthpiece with a tissue from the nightstand and switched on the phone to recognize Jerrell's voice over a static-filled connection.

"…saw Mila talking on the beach to a man Jimmy said was a narc."

"Why are we still having this conversation?" Caulfield snapped. "No Mila, no evidence. Make it look like an accident."

"There's got to be another way to handle it." Jerrell sounded indecisive. "We can't kill everyone who looks suspicious. What if she didn't even know he was a narc? We can't be sure she's trying to cut a deal—"

Carouthers jumped in again. "We *can* be sure she won't be sending us to jail if you take care of her immediately. I'm not going down. I'll cut a deal. I'll tell them that you and Rollins killed those models to cover up your operation. You know I have the proof."

Vanessa nearly dropped the phone. Jerrell and Taye had killed Gena and Bianca? She felt sick to her stomach and tears pricked her eyelids. How could she have been so wrong about Taye? Even now, she couldn't make herself believe that he'd done it. Maybe Carouthers was lying. She prayed that he was.

Jerrell actually whined. "Man, you don't have to go there. I'm handling things the best I can and I need a little help. Taye wants nothing to do with any of this."

Caulfield's voice took on a deadly note. "Have it done by tomorrow or I'm going to do some house-cleaning of my own and you won't like it. Your job should be easy with this hurricane—people disappear all the time in weather like this."

Jerrell started to speak. "Yeah, but—"

Carouthers cut him off. "Hold it a minute. I thought I heard something."

Switching off the phone and placing it back in its cradle, Vanessa dived into the closet and closed the door behind her. Seconds later, she heard the opening of the bedroom door and the footsteps of someone entering the room and moving about. When the closet door opened her breath hitched, but she was prepared.

Holding still in her spot on a shelf high above the closet floor, she felt her arms and legs trembling with the strain of maintaining her position. Despite the sound of the raging storm outside, her own breathing was loud in her ears. She prayed that Carouthers would not look up and see her.

The closet door closed and then the bedroom door did, too. Vanessa counted to twenty and eased herself down from her hiding spot. In the dark closet, she retrieved her shoes and purse from the top shelf and slipped them on, then ventured out into the bedroom again.

She had to escape from Carouthers's bedroom. Then she had to call Mackenzie and get him to pick up Mila as soon as possible.

Vanessa knelt in front of the closet door to peer outside the bedroom. Caulfield was on the phone, pacing. She was trapped.

She pulled out her cell phone. Switching it on she tried several times to call Mackenzie, but she couldn't get service. In her mind's eye, she saw Mila with her swollen face. Jerrell was going to kill her. And if he didn't, Carouthers was going to do something worse— The lights blinked and everything suddenly went dark.

She heard Caulfield cursing. He told Jerrell that he was going for the flashlight in his office. This was her chance.

Vanessa opened the door to the corridor. As she felt her way forward with a hand along the wall, she heard Caulfield rummaging in his desk. She lengthened her steps and speeded up. It was more than likely that Caulfield had an emergency lighting system that would kick in.

With a sigh of relief, she made it out of Caulfield's private suite. Still, she wasn't home free. Some of his staff would be roaming the halls and Savannah would be looking for her. Vanessa didn't dare use the penlight she had in her purse. It would be like a beacon shining in the inky blackness and telegraphing her position. Listening in the darkness, she rushed forward until she bumped into someone.

A thick, meaty hand grabbed her wrist and held on. Vanessa gasped.

Chapter 14

With a frightened shriek, Vanessa jerked her arm backward, freeing herself. In the process, she stumbled, gasping for breath. She'd had more than her share of excitement tonight.

"Are you all right?" a woman asked in Spanish.

Relief flooded Vanessa when she realized that she hadn't run into Caulfield after all. Answering in Spanish, Vanessa told the woman that she was a guest and she was lost.

"Stay here with me," the woman prompted. "You'll be fine. Mr. Carouthers has an emergency power system that should be coming on any minute."

Vanessa's sense of direction was pretty good. By her estimation, she was still far too close to Carouthers's private suite. She needed to get closer to where she was supposed to be, and she didn't have long to do it. "Thanks, but I've got to find my friends," she said, taking off.

Quite a ways down from where she'd encountered the Spanish-speaking woman, Vanessa heard someone moving about and calling her name. It was Savannah.

Answering, Vanessa found her way to the other model and made a big production about having been lost in the dark. Savannah hugged her briefly and led her back to the great room. All Carouthers's guests and the musicians were sitting in the semidarkness, huddled around the lighted candle from the table's centerpiece. No one had found anything as practical as a flashlight.

Vanessa took her seat on the couch next to Ryan.

"I was a little worried about you," he murmured as he curved an arm around her shoulders.

Vanessa refrained from stating the obvious. He had been so concerned that he had stayed in the room with the other guests instead of trying to help Savannah find her. She huddled in the curve of Ryan's arm, needing the human contact. She thought of Carouthers barking orders into the phone and ordering Mila's death. A chill crept up the back of her neck and her hands felt icy.

In the dim lighting, she glanced around the room. She remembered seeing a phone on the wall in an area of the room used to store dishes, serving trays, and silverware. Vanessa stood, and was heading toward it when Eldon Patterson's voice rang out over the buzz of conversation.

"If you're going for the phone, it's not working. We tried it already."

Vanessa tried her cell phone again. No signal.

The consummate host, Caulfield appeared with flashlights for everyone, an apology and an explanation. The storm had knocked out the power and his emergency system had failed. Since the storm outside was still battering the area and was expected to continue for several hours, they were all going to have to spend the night.

Carouthers gave each guest the option of a spot away from the storm in an inside room in the mansion to wait out the storm or a guest room with a private bath. Needing the privacy to make her call from her cell phone, Vanessa opted for the guest room.

Vanessa was happy to be shown to her room in the east wing. The large window had not yet been boarded up against the storm, but her private bath was an inside room she could escape to if and when the weather worsened. She locked the door and tried her cell phone.

She dialed Mackenzie's number and waited. Then she heard the busy-circuit recording. Vanessa dialed again and again and heard the message every time. Though frustrated, she could do little but stretch out on the bed.

Twenty minutes later, she heard a light rapping on her door. It was Ryan, trying to gain entry. Annoyed, she told him that she was tired and would see him in the morning.

He didn't insist. With him gone, she listened to the eerie crackling of the wind snapping tree branches while she dialed Mackenzie's number over and over.

It was nearly three in the morning when the call finally went through. Mackenzie sounded tired and irritable. "Where are you? I've been looking for you and so has Rollins. He called just before the storm and started to ask if I'd seen you."

She told him about waiting out the storm at Carouthers's after the dinner party and about hearing Carouthers order Jerrell to kill Mila because Jerrell had seen the model talking to a suspected narc.

Inwardly, she struggled over whether to tell Mackenzie what she'd heard about Taye and Jerrell. She wanted to wait till she had proof. She still didn't believe Taye was involved. He'd had a rough beginning and he was no angel, but the man wasn't a killer, either.

With Vanessa on the phone, he dialed an emergency DEA number and arranged for Mila to be picked up as soon as possible. The storm was expected to last another two hours.

"We've done all we can do for now," he said, once everything was set, "but there's more, isn't there?"

"Why do you say that?" She bristled, ready to argue, but knowing she had to tell all. Mackenzie amazed her with an observation that was right on target.

"Believe it or not I listen to you. I hear something different in your voice and it ain't good. C'mon, Vanessa, spill."

She told him what else she'd heard.

"Jerrell doesn't surprise me—but it's too bad about Taye. I know you really liked him."

"Do we just pull everyone in now?" she asked, hoping there'd be time to get more proof.

Mackenzie spoke grimly, his words punctuated with sighs. "We need an airtight case that involves more than hearsay. We need more of their connection to big-time drug transporting and dealing, and if Carouthers is involved, we want to make sure he can't wiggle out of it with a good lawyer. I'll order a review of all his accounts and see if we can find traces of what he's got offshore."

She bit the inside of her lip. "So I need to continue this role and do the pick up."

"Exactly, and keep your eyes and ears open." His voice took on a note of concern. "You'll be able to handle Taye?"

She was good at her job and she knew her responsibilities. She didn't hesitate. "Yes."

Agreeing to talk in the morning, they ended the call.

Outside the mansion, the storm raged violently for the rest of the night. Vanessa stayed up and tried to pull everything together in her head. Whether Annika and Guerra were involved was still unclear, but right now it seemed that Taye and Jerrell were somehow working for or with Carouthers in a drug business. Jerrell apparently handled the mules transporting the drugs. What did Taye do? Allow drug dealers to use his home for some of the distribution and help murder people who got on the wrong side of the gang?

The power returned in the morning and, as soon as she could, Vanessa said her goodbyes and made her way home. Despite bright sunshine and gor-

geous weather, driving was like running an obsta-
cle course. Downed trees, branches and power lines
were everywhere. According to the news station she
listened to in the car, six people had died in the
storm.

Vanessa called Mackenzie as soon as she could.
Some of the tension inside her eased when she heard
that the DEA had picked up Mila and put her in protective custody.

Negotiating trash, debris and some damaged cars
added an extra hour to the trip home, but she didn't
mind. She used the time to get her thoughts back on
track and prepare herself to put more emotional distance between herself and Taye.

At the complex, she parked and walked to her
unit. The grounds had taken minimal damage. Some
of the outside shutters were broken and sand, trash
and tree branches were everywhere. A downed
power line near the rear of the property was cor-
doned off with yellow caution tape.

She got a strange vibe as she inserted her condo
key in the lock and opened the door. One look and
she knew why. Taye sat on her sofa scribbling on a
pad of paper with a mechanical pencil.

At the sight of her he dropped both, an expression of such relief on his face that there was no
question that he cared for her.

"Vanessa!" He was up and at her side before she could put her purse down. He grabbed her and enveloped her in a fierce hug. Then his lips trailed from her temple to her cheek. "I was worried about you. Especially when I couldn't get ahold of you and the storm moved in so suddenly."

All thoughts of the drug gang and the murders fled. She inhaled his scent, allowed herself the comfort of his arms for several precious moments. "I didn't worry about you because I knew you had some songs to finish," she admitted. "Being an inside room with no windows, the studio has got to be one of the safest places to be in a hurricane."

"It is," he confirmed.

She dropped her arms, but he didn't seem to notice. "How did you get in here?" she asked, trying to distract him.

He chuckled close to her ear. "Some things you never forget." His fingers gently curved around the sides of her face and his mouth closed on hers.

He tasted like the chocolate mints he kept in the limo. The kiss was filled with such need that Vanessa trembled beneath waves of desire. She pushed on his chest to get a little space. "So you broke into my apartment?" she asked, stating the obvious.

"I know it sounds like a line, but I missed you,"

he continued huskily. "Then I got to thinking that if something happened to you, you'd never get the chance to tell me how much you love me."

Vanessa lifted an eyebrow. "I don't think you're ready for that," she quipped.

Taye moved closer. "Oh, I'm all ears. I'm even holding my breath."

Vanessa grinned. "Then you're a lucky man. I know CPR."

"You're a heartless witch, Vanessa."

She gave him a hard look. "You really mean 'bitch,' don't you?"

He laughed in response. "So, where were you?"

She didn't get huffy, didn't give him the attitude she gave most men trying to keep track of her activities when they didn't have the right, because the question came from genuine concern and not a need to control. This was an opportunity to find out more about Taye's relationship with Caulfield. In an even tone she told him about the party.

Taye's brown eyes bored into hers, but he'd already turned a little pale beneath his natural brown color. "You *know* Carouthers?"

"Yes. I went to school with his sister Lindy. Why?"

"He's not someone to hang with," Taye said lamely. "And despite the family fortune and connections, you shouldn't trust him."

"Why not?" she asked.

He eyed her silently, a battle obviously going on inside him. One hand released hers to form a fist. Finally, he said, "Your friend likes to live on the edge. He has more than a fascination with crime."

"He's not my friend, he's an acquaintance," she corrected. "What's going on, Taye? Tell me."

Brows furrowing, he gazed at her speculatively, then shook his head. "We shouldn't be having this conversation. Stay out of this, Vanessa, and stay away from him."

She tugged his hand. "Why? What's going on? I thought you trusted me."

"Vanessa, trusting you has nothing to do with dragging you into the shit I'm caught up in."

He was acting like a guilty man. She grabbed his arm. "You're scaring me, Taye. What kind of shit? Does this have something to do with the music business?"

"Don't be scared. It has nothing to do with you. The music business is just incidental." Dropping her hand, he moved away from her and started to pace.

"Then *what?*" she pressed. "Are you in some sort of danger?"

He turned back to face her. "If I thought that, I wouldn't be here."

"Drugs, then?"

"No." He shook his head. "I might smoke a little weed, but you know I'm not into heavy stuff."

Nothing he had said related to what she'd heard about the murders last night. With an exasperated sigh, she went to Taye, tired of trying to coax the truth out of him. "Quit dancing around the question. I'm not letting this go until you give me something to go on. Right now, this is the *only* thing we have to talk about."

"All right!" he snapped in frustration. "I'm being blackmailed."

"Blackmailed?" It wasn't what she'd been expecting to hear. "Carouthers?" He nodded and her voice dropped. "For what?"

He simply stared at her, a vulnerable, trapped look on his face. "I'm not telling you that."

"It's that bad?"

"Yeah. It's probably enough for the cops to put me away for life."

Her eyebrows went up. Connecting his words with what she knew, Vanessa figured that Taye's blackmail claim had something to do with Gena's and Bianca's gruesome murders. She'd been hoping and praying that Taye was innocent. Now, he'd just said enough to back up what she'd heard Carouthers say. She forced herself to swallow past the dryness in her throat. She needed more information.

"What *happened?*"

Taye shook his head and started back into pacing. "I don't know. I was set up—but who's going to believe that?"

"I might," she said, surprising herself. Where had those words come from? He eyed her critically and she knew she'd failed his loyalty test.

"You mean you don't already?"

"You haven't given me anything to go on," she reminded him, "but I know in my heart that you're a good person—"

"I can't talk to you about this," he said abruptly. "I've gotta go. I'll call you later." He grabbed his cell phone from the coffee table and strode to the door.

"What are you going to do?" she asked as he opened the door.

Determination hardened his face. "I'm going to handle my business."

His words sounded ominous. She hoped he wasn't planning to do something crazy, like get rid of Carouthers. "Don't do anything stupid!" she half pleaded, half demanded.

He looked angry and disappointed. "I am and I do a lot of things, Vanessa, but stupid ain't on the list." He shut the door.

"I—I didn't mean that the way it sounded," she

called after him. She ran to the door, twisted the knob and pulled it open.

Taye had already made it to the circular drive, walking fast. The limo was nowhere in sight, but he had his phone to his ear. She wanted to run after him, but what could she say? She was involved with a man who had to be knee deep in the drug business and who might have killed her friend.

Vanessa closed the door. Before she could change her mind she got on the phone and called Mackenzie to fill him in. He was certain that they were on their way to wrapping things up on the assignment.

After that, she spent an hour assuring a persistent Michelle and her parents that she was fine. Her father must have been feeling guilty, because he actually admitted to having acted hastily when he cut her off. Then he tried to sweeten things by telling her that if she came home now, all would be forgiven.

A cloud of sadness surrounded Vanessa. Years ago she'd realized that to her father, love equaled money and power. When he withheld her allowance, he was withholding his love.

He was still trying to control her.

With a heavy heart she told her father that she had to honor her commitments and then she would come back to New York.

She was on her way out for a walk on the beach when she got a call from Renee, who listened carefully while Vanessa recounted the past weeks' events, including describing her relationship with Taye. Instead of reprimanding Vanessa for jeopardizing the assignment and not calling in as instructed, Renee asked Vanessa if she thought Caulfield Carouthers could be the Duke.

Vanessa felt her eyes widen. She knew that the Governess had a theory about a person she'd nicknamed the Duke, a moneyed and well-connected individual actually pulling the strings on the money laundering, prostitution, gambling and extortion going on beneath the surface of several wealthy, influential and political circles. The way the Duke operated fit what Vanessa knew about Caulfield Carouthers.

The Duke had become a dangerous adversary for the Gotham Roses. In his most recent attack, he'd nearly killed Emma. This move had made Renee more determined than ever to bring the Duke and his organization down.

In her mind Vanessa went over and ticked off all the reasons why Caulfield could be the Duke. If he was, they would have their hands full bringing him in.

Chapter 15

After the call to him, Vanessa retrieved the pad Taye had left behind, read the words to the song he had been working on and examined the notes of accompanying music. The more she looked at it, the more she wondered about the code she'd copied from his computer. Was Taye hiding something more than his supposed involvement in the murders?

Vanessa didn't hear from Taye all day. She went to bed that night knowing that she and Mackenzie were rapidly approaching the time to wrap everything up. She'd have to make the bust soon.

An invitation and a letter arrived with the morning mail. The invitation note was from Fluffy Peters, grand dame of Palm Beach and master party thrower to the rich and famous. Slim, blond and aging beautifully with classic cheekbones, the woman was a powerhouse. It was said that more than one president's career had been made at one of Fluffy's parties. She had sent Vanessa an invitation to a huge party, her Autumn Affair, at her Palm Beach estate.

Fluffy's son had gone to Harvard with Vanessa's dad and they were still friends, so Fluffy had taken an interest in her. From the time Vanessa was an impressionable girl, she'd looked forward to Fluffy's parties. She'd never been disappointed.

The letter was from Jerrell and contained computer-printed instructions for showing up at the marina for a trip down to the Bahamas on a boat called *The Getaway* in the following week.

Recognizing the boat's name, Vanessa checked the card again. Her breath caught and her hand actually shook when she realized that *The Getaway* was Taye's boat. He'd said that he wasn't involved in drugs, yet she and others were going down to the Bahamas to pick up drugs on his boat. Another lie he'd told her…

She scanned a folded sheet of paper tucked inside the envelope with directions to a shop on Nassau where she would be given "products." All she had to do was pick up the products and bring them back to the United States. She called Mackenzie to give him the news.

He was downright jubilant. He rushed over to the condo to examine the letter and its contents and brought Erin to review the support details. Vanessa would be under surveillance from the time she picked up the packages until she brought them into the country. But would that be enough to stay safe from Jerrell…and Taye?

The night of Fluffy Peters's Autumn Affair approached without a word from Taye. It had been a full week since Vanessa had heard from him and her calls had not been returned. Vanessa was feeling stubborn, too. She didn't need him, but she did need a date for the event. Instead of pressing one of her handsome male model compatriots into escort service, she asked Mackenzie.

Fluffy's event was a formal occasion. Vanessa wore a long, sleek black Behnaz Sarafpour halter gown that dipped dangerously close to her navel and draped her breasts with just enough material for a sexy view. Stone-shaped gold and mother-of-pearl beads covered the band that curved around her neck and held up the front of the dress.

Mackenzie wore a black and charcoal Armani tuxedo.

On her four-inch Jimmy Choos, Vanessa walked into the Venetian Ballroom at the Breakers Hotel with Mackenzie and immediately immersed herself in the sights, sounds and antics that went on at one of Fluffy Peters's parties. Fluffy was a notorious snob, and the crowd was an ethnically mixed group of movers and shakers in the financial, political and entertainment arenas.

Fluffy Peters looked splendid in a glimmering, classically cut, off-the-shoulder silver Vera Wang gown that encased her slim figure and flared gently to the floor. Her blonde hair was swept up in a sophisticated swirl. Instead of kissing the air to each side of Vanessa's face, Fluffy hugged her warmly.

"I see you brought a date," she said coyly, nodding at Mackenzie.

Vanessa knew that Fluffy was gently reminding her that she could have worked the party to better advantage on her own. Where better to access a pool of the country's elite for the next boyfriend or business deal?

Vanessa introduced Fluffy to Mackenzie.

"Cody." Fluffy took Mackenzie's hand, shook it warmly and welcomed him to her party. "I'm al-

ready acquainted with the talented Cody Mackenzie," she virtually cooed.

That surprised Vanessa. How did someone like
Mackenzie get to know Fluffy Peters? Vanessa
couldn't see Fluffy having a need for a DEA agent,
and her own photographer was the only one allowed
to snap her official pictures.

Fluffy's assistant gave them printed copies of the
evening's program of events. Around them, everyone circulated with cocktails and enjoyed the five-
piece ensemble playing classical music.

Taking Vanessa and Mackenzie aside, Fluffy
said, "You know better than most how well my
parties work. In light of that, Vanessa, I reserved
your table in the best place possible. Feel free to use
or drop my name. You can thank me later!"

The best place possible? As Fluffy gracefully
melted into the crowd, Vanessa wondered what had
gotten into her. She glanced at the table, decorated
with a dramatic gold-and-white linen tablecloth. A
discreet white card with gold lettering was printed
with the words "Reserved for Vanessa Dawson and
escort."

"Just how do you know Fluffy?" she asked Mackenzie.

"Let's just say that my boss likes to hobnob with
the rich and famous," he said lamely.

"Oh, Mackenzie, you can do better than that!" she scolded.

He shook his head. "No, I can't. I wouldn't want to jeopardize an ongoing project."

At that comment, questions filled Vanessa's mind. Was Fluffy some sort of geriatric Gotham Rose? Fluffy had access to a lot of people…and a lot of secrets. Vanessa could almost see her karate chopping an astonished opponent. Fluffy was a tough old bird, well connected and intelligent, too. In fact, Fluffy fit Renee's profile of the Governess! The idea of Fluffy being the Governess intrigued Vanessa. The Governess had been after the Duke for some time, and here, within the past week or so, Vanessa had met a man who fit the bill. It was much too coincidental.

Mackenzie took her hand and placed it on his arm. "Vanessa, this is a party. Remember?"

"Of course."

"Then let's go," he said, leading her into the crowd.

At one end of the room filled with mirrored columns, vaulted ceilings and crystal chandeliers, people lined up to have their pictures taken for the society pages of the local paper. Rubi Cho, the nosy gossip columnist for the *New York Reporter*, hovered there, flitting in and out of the crowd in a red-

and-gold wrapped Marc Jacobs halter gown, to chat
with and interview the most infamous and influential of the attendees. Having been on the wrong end
of Rubi's pointed column on more than one memorable occasion, Vanessa turned and went the other
way.

She introduced Mackenzie to Tessa Vandermere,
a fellow New York heiress and friend from school,
and her date, Paul Clemmens, who was also Tessa's
broker. They chatted for a while and moved on.

Vanessa was surprised at just how many people
she knew. There were two Kennedy cousins, one of
Bush's daughters, a presidential candidate, three sen-
ators, a Saudi princess, several movie stars, Benton
Lansing the director, and many others. By tacit agree-
ment, she and Mackenzie worked the room, greeting
old friends, meeting new ones and listening in on
some of the gossip until they were ready to take their
seats.

As Vanessa sipped Crystal champagne and gave
her mouth a much-needed rest, she scanned the
room and did a shocked double take. At a table set
on an angle behind a mirrored column, but very
much in sight, Caulfield Carouthers, Jerrell Vaughn
and Taye Rollins were taking seats.

In a white Armani dinner suit, Taye Rollins was
undeniably hot. Vanessa tore her gaze away.

"Still got a thing for Rollins, eh?" Mackenzie said softly.

Not bothering to answer, Vanessa tightened her lips. Too bad they weren't close enough to hear the conversation going on at Caulfield's table. The DEA investigation into Caulfield's finances had revealed that he and Jerrell Vaughn were partners in Leisuretime Holdings, the company that owned the boat that had been used by Bianca and her friend for several trips to the Bahamas.

She and Mackenzie needed more on Caulfield to prove his connection. Deep in her heart she still clung to the hope that Taye was innocent. But based on Taye's company, was there a way for the man to look guiltier?

Their server set a fresh bottle of Crystal champagne in the canister of ice on their table. "Compliments of Ms. Peters," he said.

"Please give her our thanks," Vanessa murmured, fiddling with her nails beneath the table. Suddenly she had an idea. Why not send a bottle of champagne over to Caulfield's table in Fluffy's name? They wouldn't question the gift. She had to figure out where she could strategically place one of the jewels from the intricate false fingernails Alan Burke had designed.

Vanessa was getting up to follow the server and

make the arrangements when Rubi Cho stopped at their table.

"Vanessa," she said in a fawning tone that hid her sharp tongue, "you look absolutely fabulous in that Behnaz Sarafpour gown. Didn't I see that on a model in last year's *Vogue*?"

Wanting to smack her for being so rude, Vanessa thanked her for the compliment and acted as if she hadn't caught the catty comment. If she encouraged the woman, next Rubi would be asking how much she'd paid or if the dress was on loan.

Rubi appeared all but ready to pull up a chair and join them. "How's the photo shoot going for *Inside Sports*? Is there a chance of me getting an advance peek at the issue? For promotional purposes, of course."

Vanessa told her that the shooting in Miami was finished, but more shots were going to be done somewhere in the Caribbean. For the advance look at the magazine copy, she referred Rubi to Mackenzie.

Rubi flirted shamelessly with Mackenzie. He didn't fall under her spell, but he seemed flattered.

It seemed that Rubi was going to get her magazine exclusive. She alternately flattered and quizzed Mackenzie about his photography background and his relationship with Vanessa. "Are you sure you two aren't having a fling?" she asked more than once in her catty tone.

The first time, Vanessa told Rubi that she and Mackenzie were friends. When the question came again, she ignored it.

Unobtrusively, Vanessa glanced over at Caulfield's table. Jerrell and Caulfield were talking. Taye was morosely staring off into space. None of them seemed to have seen her and Mackenzie. Rubi had put a crimp in Vanessa's plan. Vanessa couldn't wait to get rid of the woman.

While Rubi hovered, mining all the information she could from Mackenzie, Vanessa escaped to make the arrangements for the champagne. Glancing over her shoulder, she half expected Rubi to follow her.

Once she'd arranged for champagne to be delivered in Fluffy's name, Vanessa unobtrusively planted the bug beneath the rim of the silver bucket of ice. Afterward, she stopped in the ladies' room to check her setup on the gold cell-phone receiver that Alan had given her.

Just inside the bathroom door, Vanessa stopped short. Jackie Langford, former model turned third wife to sixty-five-year-old Byron Lockheart, was at the sink in a pink Dior gown. She'd just finished doing a line of coke. Sniffing it back, she glanced up at Vanessa and smiled.

"Want some?"

Vanessa wet her lips. Her ears rang. The offer seemed to come from a distance, Jackie's voice echoing in her head. Vanessa swallowed, her mind and body remembering how good it felt to be on the drug, how long she'd been without it. She started thinking that one line, just this time, couldn't hurt. She hadn't done drugs in so long that she was utterly clean. She could—

"Vanessa?" Jackie's voice interrupted the feverish cycling of Vanessa's thoughts.

Her eyes focused on Jackie. This time she saw and heard her clearly. Jackie's pupils were dilated and her voice was already a little slurred from the drug. Her nose looked swollen and a bit of blood was smeared on the corner of one nostril. "It's good stuff," Jackie assured her.

Instead of Jackie, Vanessa saw herself, strung out and skinny as a scarecrow. "I—I'll pass," Vanessa managed to say in a voice that revealed none of the soul-stealing desire she still felt for the drug. She could almost hear it calling her name and promising to give her everything she'd ever wanted. Blinking, she rejected the illusion and gathered herself. The drug was bad for her, mentally, physically and emotionally.

Vanessa stepped past Jackie to enter one of the

spacious stalls and lock the door. Propped against the wall, she hugged herself and forced deep breaths in and out. Once Vanessa heard Jackie exiting the powder room, she let herself relax.

Leaning against the wall inside the stall, Vanessa turned on her gold cell phone and tuned it to the frequency of the bug she'd planted. The bug and her cell-phone receiver worked like a charm. She heard Jerrell bragging to Caulfield and Taye about the hot night he'd had with one of the models. Surprisingly, Caulfield and Taye seemed as unimpressed as Vanessa.

Returning to the Venetian Ballroom, Vanessa sat at the table with her cell-phone receiver and listened to the conversation at Caulfield's table. With his receiver tuned to the same frequency, Mackenzie discreetly listened in, too.

Taye seemed angry with Jerrell and Caulfield. He was silent more often than not, but when he spoke, his comments were caustic. When Benton Lansing joined them at the table, the conversation became more of a meeting.

They talked about the coming trip to the Bahamas. Everyone but Benton was going. They'd scheduled a bunch of models to "make it look good" and "move things along." Taye was silent until they started listing the models. When Vanessa's name came up, Taye was furious. He accused Jerrell of deliberately going after his girlfriend. Then he insisted that they take her name off the list.

Jerrell seemed to enjoy baiting Taye. Not amused, Caulfield and Benton tried to keep Jerrell and Taye from drawing too much attention. When Taye ordered Jerrell to put Vanessa down as a private guest instead of a mule, Jerrell told him that he would have to check with Vanessa first. Taye looked as if he would have kicked Jerrell's ass right there, but Caulfield and Benton insisted that Taye go cool off before he got himself forcibly removed.

Standing, Taye strode away from the table. From her vantage point, Vanessa saw him head for the terrace. Her heart went with him.

Back at the table Caulfield asked Jerrell, "Why is that heiress on your list anyway? Her family has plenty of money."

"Yeah, but that's their money and it's all about control," Jerrell corrected him. "They've cut her off because they don't want her modeling and she needs money to tide her over till she gets paid for the magazine deal."

Caulfield nodded. "Okay. You'd better rein your boy in. This shit is getting old. His ass is already in a sling and we've got to put up with his pouting, too?

If he keeps this up, I'll throw his ass off the boat in the middle of the ocean myself!"

Jerrell's voice turned edgy. "You threatening me, too?"

"No, Jerrell, you act like you know who's in charge. Play your cards right and I might get you a copy of the rest of the video. I'm talking about the part of the tape that shows what happened before you and Taye woke up looking guilty." Caulfield laughed out loud. It was a nasty sound.

"You mean you got a tape of everything?" Jerrell asked, hope creeping into his voice.

"Oh yeah." Caulfield drained his glass and set it on the table.

The server rushed forward to pour him another glassful of champagne and then returned to a spot a discreet distance from the table.

"I'm a good manager. I believe in finding ways to motivate the people who work for me and with me," Caulfield declared. "Making that tape was a unique opportunity to make an example of those models and restore order, and to force you and Rollins into line."

Vanessa and Mackenzie shared a glance. She swallowed bile and chased it down with champagne. Caulfield Carouthers was some piece of work.

Vanessa set her glass down. Deep inside she

imagined Carouthers on his knees in prison, busy licking big Bubba's boots. It was a helluva goal, but she was going for it.

Chapter 16

Anger made Vanessa too restless to sit. She scanned the crowd for people she'd missed her first time around the room. Noticing that dinner was now being served on the other side of the ballroom, she stood on the sidelines talking to people and watching the band.

Food was the last thing on her mind and she didn't feel she could keep anything down. Tonight, she'd heard enough to make her forever grateful for the Gotham Roses and the government agencies they worked with. People like Caulfield Carouthers deserved to be caught and put away for life.

She didn't know what to think of Taye anymore, but it sounded as though he'd been framed. *Sure,* her inner voice chided. *Does that mean that he's* just *a drug dealer and not a murderer?*

Someone called her name and she turned away from the band to answer. It was Taye.

"Vanessa, I thought I recognized you standing over here. I should have known you'd be here, it being a high-society affair and all." He stepped close and took her hand.

An electric current went through her. When his warm lips brushed her cheek, sparks flew. Vanessa closed her eyes for a moment.

"You look hot. I couldn't have dreamed it better myself." Taye's eyes darkened, taking on a hungry, daring look. "All this attraction we've got for each other, Vanessa, and we keep wasting it. What's up with that? How come we're not somewhere wearing each other out? You're into me as much as I'm into you."

She wet her lips. Wrong move. He focused on her mouth. "Maybe we've both gotten old enough to think about it first," she said.

"But I *have* been thinking about it, Vanessa. I know there's a strong, intelligent woman beneath your beautiful face, that gorgeous body and the family money."

Vanessa struggled with her emotions. She wanted to say something similar, but couldn't. Soon he'd probably hate her guts.

"So maybe I'm ahead of you when it comes to us being together. I was mad at you for not trusting me, so I stayed away."

He was going to kiss her. Vanessa saw him leaning in. She also saw the covert looks they were getting. One did not kiss out in the open at one of Fluffy's parties unless one wanted to end up as fodder for the gossip columns and grant them the gift of a candid shot. A couple of cameras flashed.

When Vanessa spotted Rubi Cho bearing down on them like a homing pigeon, it was the last straw. "Dance with me," she ordered, heading for the ballroom floor and dragging him along.

In the middle of the crowd they danced to an old Gershwin tune and relaxed in each other's arms. The next song was an instrumental version of the Temptations song, "Just My Imagination." Taye kept the fancy footwork to a minimum.

"I want you to come to the Bahamas as my personal guest next week," he insisted as they danced around the floor.

This was the opening she had been looking for. She needed to hear Taye's side of things. "I've already gotten my invitation," she said lightly, "so I'll be there."

The hand at her back curled around her waist in a silent admonishment. "I know about your money problems. That's why I was glad we still needed someone for the video. You were the one I wanted anyway and I knew that you really needed the work."

"So you asked me to be in your video just to help me out?" she asked. He'd just managed to take the shine off one of the most memorable jobs in her career.

"Vanessa, no. *No.* I just made sure that the terms were extra good for you and I called off my top dog, Mike the shark, and told them not to fight it."

That sounded less like she'd been a charity case. "Okay," she said agreeably. "What are we really talking about?"

"I want you to be my personal guest on the cruise."

"What difference does it make?"

"A lot and you know it." He speared her with a glance. "The models with invitations from Jerrell will be taking chances. They could end up getting arrested. I don't want you involved in that."

"So you're trying to rescue me from Jerrell's scheme?"

"Yeah, something like that."

"Why don't you rescue all of the girls?"

"Because you're the one I care about."

"But you could tell Jerrell that he can't do that on your yacht."

"No, I can't. Remember what we talked about last week? I've been literally throwing money into a hole and risking everything I've worked for. Sometimes I think it would be better to just give up and let them cart me off to jail, and then I think about how much I don't want that bastard to win. I'm working a plan to get him off my back and out of my life."

"Jerrell?" she asked, wanting to clarify.

"No, Caulfield. Jerrell's sort of a pawn, too, but he has less for Caulfield to take and he handles being blackmailed a lot better than I do."

"You're not going to do anything permanent to Caulfield…."

Taye stopped dancing for a moment. "I'm getting rid of him," he assured her. "I'm going to hit him where it hurts, the pocket. I've been working on getting the numbers to the accounts he uses for his work, and every now and then I hear something about a tape that proves I'm innocent. I want a copy."

So do I, Vanessa thought. As far as she was concerned, the tape would clear up a lot of issues, legal and personal.

"So you'll do the cruise as my guest," he prodded as the song ended.

She shook her head. "I gave my word to Jerrell. Besides, I need the money for the repairs on the condo Grandma left me."

Taye frowned at her. "You wouldn't lose anything. I'd give you the damn money!"

She frowned back. "I didn't ask you for money. I'd rather get my own," she countered stubbornly. "I can do this. You can't rescue the world, Taye."

"I was trying to rescue you," he snapped back.

"And I just turned you down."

He threw her a frustrated look. "You don't know what you're dealing with."

The music faded and they headed for the edge of the dance floor. "You came with a date?" he asked, glancing around. "Stupid question," he amended, seeing her expression. "Where are you sitting?"

She showed him the table where Mackenzie was still sitting with his cell phone glued to his ear. He was surprised that they hadn't seen each other, until she pointed out the angle of table and the mirrored pole.

A new voice interrupted their conversation. "Taye Rollins, I was hoping I'd get a chance to meet you here!"

Vanessa shrank inwardly. Rubi Cho again. What had Vanessa done to merit such dedicated attention? There were at least two hundred other people in the ballroom for Rubi to hound.

Rubi's eyes positively sparkled as she acknowledged Vanessa. "Vanessa, you *do* get around," she murmured. "I've been watching you two from the sidelines. I get such a kick out of watching lovebirds."

"We're good friends," Vanessa said quickly, hoping Taye would take the hint.

Ignoring her, Rubi moved in to quiz Taye on how he'd met Vanessa and if they'd come to the event together.

Standing there listening to Rubi mine information out of a man in her life for the second time in one evening grated on Vanessa's nerves, but her anger and annoyance were things Rubi would relish and use to her advantage.

Vanessa was happy when the conversation switched to Taye's latest release and a new group he was promoting. Excusing herself, Vanessa noted that dinner was now being served on their side of the room as she returned to her table.

Mackenzie set his cell phone on the table when she came back. "I see you found the Hot T," he quipped.

"He found me," she replied. "And so did Rubi Cho."

Cody chuckled. "There must be a story in the air. That woman has a nose for it. What do you think? Love between the poor model heiress and the hip-hop mogul?"

She shot him a withering glance. "We're not going there, Mackenzie. There're too many questions to be answered." She pointed to his cell phone. "Hear anything else worth mentioning?"

"Other than that they're not happy with Taye, and Caulfield's about ready to throw him overboard?" Mackenzie pressed the record button, folded the phone and placed it in his pocket.

At a loss, Vanessa shook her head. "I don't know how to respond to that, Mackenzie. It's been a hell of an evening."

He extended a hand across the table to pat hers. "Just get ready, 'cause this little trip you're taking will be far from boring."

Minutes later, Taye surprised Vanessa and Mackenzie by joining them at their table for dinner. It raised a few eyebrows at some of the other tables and cameras flashed, but Mackenzie was fine with it. There had never been any animosity between the two men.

After dinner, Vanessa danced alternately with

Mackenzie and Taye and a few friends. She gave the performance of her life when Caulfield made his rounds and found her on the dance floor. He danced like a professional, but with everything she knew about him, it took a lot of energy for her to smile and follow his lead.

At the end of the evening she hugged Fluffy and thanked her for a wonderful party that had been both entertaining and "informative." The old girl smiled and winked at her.

Although Mackenzie had escorted her to the party, he agreed to let Taye take her home.

Vanessa's sense of propriety prompted her to at least put up a token protest, but she decided not to waste the energy. She really needed some time with Taye and there was no telling how much longer they'd be able to see one another.

Behind the privacy glass in the back of Taye's limousine, she reclined against the leather seats with a tension headache.

"Don't worry, I'm not going to ask you to perform," Taye whispered. He placed a kiss on her temple.

"That's not funny," she whispered back. She felt him fumbling with her shoes and taking them off.

"Beautiful shoes," he murmured, "but not too practical."

He massaged her tired, aching feet with strong fingers that curved around her heels and smoothed the delicate arch. He definitely knew what he was doing. A sigh of pleasure escaped her lips. Encouraged, his fingers slid up to her ankles and calves to knead the flesh.

"Mmm." She moaned low in her throat. "Where'd you learn to do this?"

"You don't want to know." His voice was husky and urgent. He pushed the expensive dress out of the way. Wonderfully thorough hands manipulated the flesh on her thighs, urging her to relax and splay them open.

"Yes, I do!" she said, her sentence ending at a high pitch when she felt his warm lips on her thigh.

He placed moist, tender kisses on the soft flesh, just above the lace edge of her thigh-high stockings. "Girls 101, courtesy of Maurice, the ladies' man in the gang," he said, his mouth moving against her skin in another variation of a kiss. "Of course I had a few ideas of my own."

Vanessa shivered and squirmed beneath his expert attention. Suddenly he was tracing the edges of her tiny gold-lace bikinis with his tongue and cupping her heat with one big hand. "Oh, Vanessa," he said hoarsely, "We've crossed over into my favorite fantasy. Now I've got the real thing."

She undulated against him, one hand gripping his muscular shoulder beneath the evening suit and the other curling in his thick hair. Her stomach tightened and her breath came in little pants. She was starting to melt.

Apparently sensing it, he hooked his fingers into the thin lace and ripped them down. Carefully holding her legs, he showered her with lingering kisses. Then he moved in to cover her with his mouth and lovingly administer the deepest, most gloriously intimate kiss she'd ever received.

Losing control, she experienced a full-scale volcanic meltdown, right against him on the seat. Afterward, she lay there, too weak to move. Holding her, he lay with her, unconcerned about wrinkling his suit or getting it wet. Her headache was definitely gone.

When they arrived at her condo, she caught the mischievous look on his face as he slipped her panties into his pocket. Flattered but not sure she was going to let him get away with it, she caught his hand. "Is that for the private collection?"

"There is no underwear collection, but I'm up for starting one just for you. I thought I could put them with my autographed copies of the Sweetheart Dreams Catalog," he answered with a straight face.

Good answer. Locking her arms around his neck,

Vanessa pressed herself against him and kissed him passionately.

He slowly pulled away. "I want to be with you, Vanessa. Invite me to stay. It's what we both want."

His words emboldened her. She was the one holding them back—but was it wrong to want his name cleared before they went further? "I want you, Taye. That's the truth. I'm not playing games."

His wise eyes seemed to see her thoughts. "You think I'm a drug dealer…or worse?"

"That's *not* what I think," she answered quickly. "But this time I can't go on my instincts. There's too much at stake."

A vulnerable look flashed across his face, then his expression hardened. He was about to turn away from her.

She closed a hand on his muscular arm, hating that she'd hurt him and that he was putting on a front for her. "You don't understand! I—I've never felt this way about anyone."

He searched her face. "You're scared?"

She nodded, realizing it was the truth.

"I am, too," he muttered, closing his eyes and rubbing his forehead against hers. "There's you and then there's the big mess I'm trying to get out of. Give me some time. I'll find a way."

Chapter 17

The next morning Vanessa bought a copy of the *New York Reporter* on her way back from the gym. Thumbing through the pages, she stopped to read the Rubi Cho column, and it was everything thing she'd dreaded.

What model real estate heiress cut off from the family funds was seen partying in a gorgeous black Behnaz Sarafpour halter gown with not one, but two dates at Fluffy Peters's Autumn Affair in Palm Beach? One of the favored dates was Cody Mackenzie, hunky photographer on the *Inside Sports* Swimsuit Fantasy shoot. Bachelor number two was none other than bad-boy hip-hop producer/artist/clothing designer, Taye Rollins aka Hot T. Love was in the air.

Groaning in dismay, Vanessa made her way back to the condo. When she arrived the phone was ringing. She didn't need the caller ID to tell her who it was. She lifted the receiver.

"Hello Mama."

To her credit, her mother spent the first five minutes of the call calmly inquiring about Vanessa's health. Then she moved in for the kill. "Have you seen today's *New York Reporter?* What's going on with you, Vanessa? You've had your share of controversial boyfriends, but you've never resorted to thugs!"

Vanessa took issue with the statement and told her that Taye was not a thug.

"Okay, criminal, then!" her mother corrected. "And I read somewhere that he's been shot at least twice."

Vanessa defended Taye. "All of that was a long time ago, Mama. He was a wild kid and he got involved with a gang."

"So he's not involved with gangs now?"

Vanessa blew out a heavy breath. "Not in the same way. He produces and sponsors a lot of new groups. Some of them come from gangs."

"Vanessa, we have such high hopes for you. Having someone like that for a boyfriend is bad enough, but if you're thinking of marrying him, your father might be angry enough to cut you off permanently."

Vanessa had had enough. She opened her mouth and the words poured out in an acidic stream. "To tell you the truth, Mama, he's not my boyfriend and I'm not thinking of marrying anyone, but I'm really getting sick and tired of being threatened every time I do something you and Daddy don't like or understand. You're never on my side."

"That's not true!" her mother exclaimed.

"Yes, it is." Vanessa flung the words at her. "Mama, I'm not your little girl anymore. I'm trying to stand on my own two feet and do something with my life. What's wrong with that? Having a lot of money shouldn't give you and Daddy the right to control me forever."

"Vanessa, you know we want you to have the best life has to offer." Her mother's voice shook. "Everything we do is done out of love for you."

"Then can't you *show* me some love by supporting me in the things I want to do? You and Dad are never there when I really need you." Vanessa was on a roll, telling her mother all the things she'd previously confined to her dreams, and it was liberating.

"I'm not taking any more abuse from you," her mother cried, ending the connection.

Vanessa realized that she was crying. She felt like scum for upsetting her mother. Her mother could be snooty and bossy, but it was true that she was always trying to do what she thought was best for her family.

Vanessa placed the phone back in the cradle. Three minutes later, it rang again. This time it was Michelle, angry that Vanessa had upset her mother. Michelle was also sure that Vanessa had destroyed any chance she would have of modeling.

"Michelle," she began, "nothing I do has any impact on whatever you want to do in life. If you want to be a model, there's absolutely nothing our parents can do to stop you when you're eighteen. If I mess up, I mess up *my* life. I can't be responsible for yours, too." When Michelle argued and complained about not being able to make an early start, Vanessa said, "You know Mom and Dad love you. When they see that you're not going to give up, they'll probably make some sort of arrangement. Don't give up on your dream, baby. If there's anything I can do to help, I'll do it."

It took another twenty minutes to get Michelle

calmed down. Vanessa replaced the phone feeling like she'd been in a boxing ring. Between the family conflict, the relationship with Taye and tomorrow's trip to the Bahamas, she felt on edge. One mistake and she could end up like Gena and Bianca.

The day of the cruise down to the Bahamas arrived. Knowing that Taye had spent the night on his boat, Vanessa got there extra early to have breakfast with him before the scheduled departure.

Her first hint of a problem was the acrid scent of smoke in the air as she walked along the dock. Then she saw it. Orange-and-black flames shooting out of a blackened area of *The Getaway*.

For once, she was glad that she wasn't wearing the heels she loved. In her sensible sand-colored deck shoes, Vanessa picked up her suitcase and ran toward the yacht. She mentally skimmed through what she remembered about the layout of the boat. The fire had to be in or close to the master suite where Taye slept.

She looked for Taye around the yacht and on the open deck. A lot of the boats were gone already. There was no one around except an old man in white shorts and a loud Hawaiian-print shirt. He looked every bit of eighty-five and was standing on the dock next to the boat, using a garden hose in a fruitless attempt to douse the flames shooting out of the cabins. It was like using a child's water gun.

"Taye?" she called out, frantically searching again. She addressed the old man. "Have you seen Taye Rollins?"

"He's usually not here until much later," the old man yelled. "So the boat's probably empty. I heard somebody running out on the dock this morning and a crashing noise. I looked out 'cause I thought someone threw a rock or something. Didn't see 'em, though. I was on my way out here to rinse off my deck when I saw the flames. It hasn't been long since it started. I've already called the fire department—they should be here soon. I was trying to keep it from spreading...."

Feeling panicky, Vanessa had been unconsciously helping the old man finish his sentences. Now she dropped her case, thanked him and turned back to the yacht. Taye *was* on the yacht. He had to be. Her chest felt heavy at the thought.

She gathered the length of her hair in one hand, twisted it and stuffed it under the baseball cap she kept in her bag. The she dipped her cotton jacket into the water and climbed on board. A wall of heat met her. The old man was yelling something, but she ignored him. Blinking, she pushed herself forward through the open doors of the main salon.

Hadn't she read somewhere that boats burned quickly because they contained petroleum products? With the wet jacket covering her nose, she ran through the galley and down the passage toward the master suite.

As she'd expected, fire raged there. It was hot enough to redden the surface of her skin. She couldn't even get close. "Taye!" she called out, hoping to hear a reply.

Running to the deck, she found a pole and rushed back toward the master suite with it. She planted her feet and pounded and prodded the door. The persistent picture in her mind was of Taye inside, unconscious or dead.

The door stayed shut. Hearing nothing but the eerie crackling sound of the fire, she headed back to the galley in defeat. If Taye was in the master suite, she couldn't get to him on her own. She coughed, her eyes tearing in the thick smoke. She was running out of time.

She mentally kicked herself when she spotted the fire extinguisher on a hook in the galley. It wasn't big enough to put out the fire, but she could save Taye if he was anywhere but the bedroom. On a wild hope, she ran with it back to the living area where the large-screen television was located.

Taye was stretched out on the sofa, facedown.

Lowering her head in the smoke-filled area, Vanessa dropped the fire extinguisher and went to him. *Dear Lord, please don't let him be dead!*

Crouching in the smoke, she shook his shoulder, yelling out his name. His skin felt warm. He groaned. *Good. He's alive.* Tugging with both hands, she rolled him over on the scorched carpet and shook him hard. There was something wrong. Smoke inhalation?

He was mumbling something. Encouraged, Vanessa heard her name. "We've got to get out of here now," she insisted. When it looked as if he was slipping away again, she slapped him.

Taye blinked. "Why'd you do that?" he growled. He started coughing and hacking in the acrid fumes. She covered his nose and mouth with the other end of her wet jacket.

Vanessa looked back toward the master suite. The fire was spreading. Pretty soon, the area they were in would be engulfed in flames. "We've got to go now. I can't carry you. You've got to help me, Taye."

She rolled him onto the floor. He grumbled at the impact, but seemed a bit more alert. She wondered if he'd taken something to make him sleep. Alternately ordering, begging, pleading and cajoling, she got him up from the floor. He leaned on her heavily, barely able to walk.

Grunting under the strain, Vanessa found herself thanking Jimmy Valentine for all the extra weight and endurance training he'd insisted on. With an eye on the encroaching flames, they inched their way toward the open deck.

She heard the high-pitched whine of fire engines. *Dear Lord, yes!* She didn't have time to wait, but maybe, just maybe, someone could help her get Taye off the boat.

It took forever to get him to the open deck. Vanessa surveyed the area through teary, smoke-filled eyes. Two firemen were on the dock hooking up their firehose. Two more in protective suits were climbing aboard.

She sagged, glad that help had finally arrived. One of the firemen bent to lift Taye in a fireman's carry.

"I'm okay. I can get down by myself," Vanessa told the other fireman.

Both men worked together to get the gangway down and carry Taye off the yacht. Black smoke and sweat formed a tarlike substance on her skin. Bone-tired, Vanessa pushed one leg in front of the other until she reached the bottom of the gangway.

Two heavy streams of water were already working to douse the flames. Away from the boat, the emergency technicians already had Taye on a stretcher with a tube down his throat. They were giving him oxygen.

She headed for him, anxious to make sure he wasn't hurt. He wasn't moving and he didn't seem to be conscious. *Had the smoke injured his lungs?* But the emergency technicians made her lie down on one of the stretchers and insisted that she take oxygen, too. She was soon breathing more easily, but realized that both her throat and chest were sore.

The flames were nearly out now, but the once-beautiful yacht was a burnt shadow of what it had once been. She looked up and saw Jerrell Vaughn and one of Taye's new hip-hop artists in the crowd standing on the dock. No one was scheduled to be at the boat for another couple of hours. She couldn't shake the feeling that they'd had something to do with the fire.

Vanessa left the hospital with Taye, both of them still smelling of smoke. She felt okay, but they both still had sore throats and hoarseness. The doctor had wanted to keep Taye for observation, but nothing kept Taye Rollins down for long. He'd accepted some pain medication for his throat and chest and some throat lozenges, and had promised to not smoke or go out in cool weather until his symptoms had eased.

Vanessa was anxious to get to the Bahamas to do

her pick up. Mackenzie had called to tell her that the other models had left for the Bahamas hours ago aboard another yacht, *The Venture*. He also said that the investigation into Caulfield's finances had yielded the fact that Caulfield owned a lot of stock in Taye's record company.

As they climbed into the back of the limousine, Vanessa told Taye about seeing Jerrell and one of the hip-hop artists on the dock while she and Taye were being taken to the hospital.

Taye settled beside her on the seat. "Yeah, Jerrell dropped by the hospital to make sure I was all right before he took off for the Bahamas."

That sounded innocuous. "They weren't supposed to be down at the boat for another hour," she said carefully. "What if they had something to do with the fire on the boat?"

Taye looked at her, shaking his head. "I like you worrying about me, but Jerrell's like a brother to me. He's got my back and I've got his. It's been that way since we were kids."

This time Vanessa shook her head. She wanted to explore her suspicions with Taye. "Yeah, but…"

"No 'buts' Vanessa. I know where Jerrell is coming from," he insisted. "Now I've got a ticket on a speedboat charter to the Bahamas. So I've got to get going. It leaves in about three hours."

"Let me come with you." Vanessa touched his arm.

"No. You know how I feel about you working for Jerrell," he insisted.

"And you know how I feel about making my own decisions," she interjected.

Resigned, Taye shook his head. "Can you make the charter?"

Vanessa nodded. She was already packed. She only needed to shower and get the smoke out of her hair.

Holding hands and cuddling in the back of the limousine with Taye, she realized just how much he meant to her. The image of him stretched out and unmoving on the cushions aboard the yacht was imprinted on her brain. She would do everything she could to help him prove his innocence.

Chapter 18

At Taye's rented mansion in the Bahamas that night, Vanessa came down the marble staircase to party in her daring Viktor & Rolf black-lace mini-dress. For modesty's sake, a black band accented her waist and hid the skimpy flesh-colored panties sewn into the dress. The black lace provided a peekaboo view of her body and made it appear that she was completely nude underneath. With a wide smile, she took the stairs slowly in her gold Jimmy Choos, aware that, for once, she really didn't want to party.

Mackenzie had arrived with news that arson was suspected in the fire on Taye's boat. It was no surprise for Vanessa. Seeing Jerrell in the crowd made her suspicious. No matter how hard she'd tried, she hadn't been able to get Taye to talk about what had happened.

Taye was waiting for her at the bottom of the steps. His eyes lit up at the sight of her and scanned her outfit. "Hello, beautiful," he said, taking her hand when she neared the bottom. "That's one hot dress you're wearing. Makes me want to drag you back upstairs."

She thanked him for the compliment. Her dress had been jokingly described as a "fuck-me dress" when she negotiated to borrow it from the designers.

Taye wore a white-on-white suit from the Taye-Wear clothing line. It had a double-breasted jacket and baggy pants. Prada shoes covered his feet and his hair was freshly cut. He looked like a dream—except for the weariness behind his smile.

Before she knew it, he'd led her to the huge livingroom's hardwood floor. He whirled her out and back in a slow dance. If it hadn't been for glaring stares from Jerrell and Carouthers, the moment would have been wonderful. As they finished the dance, she saw Mackenzie, standing at the appetizers, watching them. Taye had invited him to the party.

Vanessa circulated and made a good show of enjoying the party. She spent time with Annika and her friend, Bridgette. Annika had promised Jerrell that she would give Vanessa some tips on picking up the product without looking suspicious and on getting back without attracting too much attention. Vanessa hid her surprise that she had been right about Annika after all.

When Annika took off to dance with Benton Lansing, Vanessa watched and wondered. Was everyone at the party a part of the drug activities?

Caulfield came over to Vanessa. She didn't trust him. Tall, urbane and charming, he kissed her cheek and drew her into his arms to dance. "How's the family?"

"They're fine," she answered hiding her hatred for the man. "You know Daddy just closed on an old hotel in New York. It's being converted into condos."

"Your father always did have quite a knack for real estate," he remarked, executing a series of skillful movements. "How is your lovely mother?"

"Oh, she's fine. She just left for a spa in Arizona, getting the works."

"And your darling sister, Michelle?"

"She's at a summer camp in upstate New York. She wanted to concentrate on her horsemanship."

"How charming," he responded.

"What about your family?" she asked politely continuing the charade. "What's Lindy up to?"

Caulfield wrinkled his nose. "Lindy is about to marry someone totally unsuitable."

"Who?" Vanessa asked in surprise.

"Our chauffeur's son."

Stunned, Vanessa tried to imagine Lindy going against her family's wishes. She'd never seen it happen. "How's the rest of your family?" she asked diplomatically.

"We'll be a lot better when the chauffeur's son is out of the picture," Carouthers said. Amusement glinted in his eyes as he watched her carefully. "I hear that your family is not happy that you're back modeling."

"No, they're not."

"To the point that they've cut you off from the family allowance?" he pushed.

"Yes." Vanessa looked down. "Modeling is all I have for now."

Caulfield patted her shoulder. "Sorry, Vanessa. I just wanted you to know that if you ever need help, you can count on me."

Vanessa met his gaze. "Thank you. I appreciate it."

His questions were enough to make her wonder if they'd somehow become suspicious of her.

On the dance floor, Caulfield's moves were smooth and coordinated. Vanessa had to work hard to maintain her friendly, easygoing facade because every time she looked at the man, she recalled his comments about the models' murders and the cold-blooded reasoning behind it. Caulfield Carouthers was about as charming as a snake. When he finally moved on, Vanessa sat down. Her jaw ached from smiling so much and her nerves were taut.

Mackenzie brought her a glass of wine and drew her out onto the veranda. The strong scent of marijuana rode the wind. "Relax, Vanessa, the night's still young," he said as she gulped her drink.

"You're not the one who just spent almost half an hour being friendly and acting as if everything was peachy with Caulfield Carouthers!" she snapped.

"While you were charming the rat, Taye got a phone call and I swear he looked like someone had killed his dog. He went off by himself for a few minutes and now he's back, trying to act like everything's okay."

She told him about Annika and he nodded, not seeming surprised at all. Unless something went wrong with the pick up, everyone, including Annika, would be arrested when they tried to bring the drugs into the United States.

Back inside, Vanessa drank another glass of wine. On her way to the bathroom, she stopped short at the sight of two guests doing coke on the enclosed deck. She stared.

I can't go on like this, she acknowledged inwardly as she continued on.

It can't give you anything you don't already have, a voice in her head reminded her.

In the bathroom she studied her reflection in the mirror for several minutes. She'd come a long way from the young model who'd gotten pulled into the fast life and had had to be rescued. Now she could rescue herself. She wasn't going to let herself fall back into old habits—she was strong enough to fight her addiction, no matter what happened.

Massaging her forehead, she acknowledged that she was here by choice. She was in control and she had a job to do. That meant getting through tonight, doing the pick up tomorrow and bringing the product into the country. The DEA would do the rest.

After wiping the perspiration off her nose, she patted her face with a damp towel and redid her makeup. Another hour and she could leave the party.

Someone knocked on the bathroom door. Gathering her things, she opened it. It was Taye.

"You're not hiding out in here, are you?" he whispered.

"What do you think?" she asked.

Blocking her path, he stepped forward and nudged her back into the bathroom and locked the door. In a split second his mouth was on hers, warm, wet and exciting. He tasted like cognac.

"I've been waiting all evening to do this," he murmured.

Eyes closed, she reveled in the solid warmth of his muscular body. His hands slid beneath the black lace to caress her skin and his hot mouth covered her breast, lace and all. Vanessa moaned low in her throat.

His hands fastened on the skimpy panties sewn into the dress and slipped inside to caress her intimately. "I was wondering," he chuckled. "Feeling a little freaky? I've got a few hot fantasies about you, me and a bathroom counter." He lifted her up on the counter and stepped between her legs.

Vanessa pushed on his chest and rubbed her forehead against his. "After everything we've been through today, I'm really tempted," she admitted. "But I'd rather have the bed and I don't want to rush."

"I can't leave the party for more than a few minutes right now," he admitted.

She caressed his wide shoulders and his back. "I thought I'd lost you this morning."

"I thought it was the end, too." He kissed her hard. "I'll never forget how you saved my life."

"Taye, someone set that fire."

"I know. One minute I was having a drink, and the next, it's daylight and the boat's burning. I couldn't get my head together, I could hardly move. I think Caulfield's trying to get rid of me. He's been buying the record company stock with drug and blackmail money. If I disappear or die, he could take over everything, easy. He's got Jerrell sewed up."

She released a long breath. "And if Jerrell set the fire?"

Taye shook his head. "I've been trying to work my way out of Caulfield's latest scheme," he continued. "Right now, everything's up in the air. I had my whiz computer boy find the number of his account in a Grand Cayman bank. That's where he's stashing the cash. I told you that Caulfield set me and Jerrell up for blackmail, but I didn't tell you how. We were having a couple of drinks at his place and suddenly, we woke up next to a couple of dead models. Caulfield filmed the whole thing. He showed us the tape, and, if my mother saw the tape, she'd swear I was guilty. He had somebody kill those women. I knew Caulfield was crazy, but this was over the top."

"Did you know those models?" Vanessa asked, tensing as she waited for the answer.

"They'd been on the boat and to some of the parties," Taye admitted. "They were involved in Jerrell's scheme, too."

How could Taye put up with Jerrell's antics? The words tumbled out, her tone revealing too much of her feelings: "How could you let Jerrell run something like that right under your nose?"

There was a note of warning in his eyes. He wasn't going to take any verbal abuse from her. "I'm not stupid, Vanessa, and you weren't born yesterday. At first it was just Jerrell having his own stuff and some people wanting in on it during a party. You've seen the exposés about the entertainment industry. It's real. You know that up close and personal, don't you?"

She swallowed, not liking the way this was going.

He touched her cheek. "Nothing personal, but some people can't do without their drugs. The next thing I know, Jerrell's got a side business going with Caulfield, and when I went to put a stop to it, Caulfield set up the blackmail scheme."

"He killed those models just to blackmail you and Jerrell?" she asked incredulously.

"No." He rubbed his face against hers. "Some of

the product they were moving came up missing and they couldn't pay for it. Jerrell can be a thug, but he never killed anyone. Caulfield took over and killed them as a lesson to the rest of the mules. They're all scared of him now."

Vanessa traced his dark eyebrows with her thumbs. "So what are you going to do now?"

"Try to get some sort of deal with the police or the DEA."

She laid her head on his padded chest. "What do you have to bargain with?" she asked, fighting the desire to tell him everything.

"Tapes of him gloating about the blackmail, giving orders and planning trips for the drug business, and his numbered bank account in the Caymans."

It probably wasn't enough to keep Taye from doing time, and they both knew it. But Vanessa kept the thought to herself.

Then Taye told her that he'd been secretly meeting with one of Caulfield's men and had learned of a tape that showed everything, even the models' murders. He'd paid money, and was supposed to get a copy of the tape within a day or so, but tonight he'd learned that his contact had been shot at a nightclub in Miami.

Vanessa closed her eyes. She had leads on how and why the models had died, and had pretty much identified the top of the drug ring. There was a strong possibility that Carouthers was the Duke. Tomorrow they'd bring them down. Another successful assignment, nearly complete, and yet she was so depressed.

They left the bathroom reluctantly. Vanessa headed up the stairs to bed and Taye said goodnight to his guests.

In his bedroom they lay together on chocolate-colored silk sheets. Taye gathered her close, nudging her with his erection. The feel of his hard, warm body against hers made her dizzy with pleasure.

He licked her lips. His tongue dipped deep into her mouth, swirling, sliding, teasing. She leaned into him, putting everything she'd been holding back into the wonder of exploring his mouth.

Taye's low moan shattered what was left of her inhibitions. She sat up, fumbling with hidden fasteners and more than anxious to get out of the dress. Helping her, he hooked his fingers into the lace and slid it upward past her thighs, over her curving hips and away from the soft mounds of her breasts. She lifted her arms and tilted her chin up, and the dress came up over her head. He tossed it across the room.

"Vanessa!" Taye's eyes smoldered and his voice was hoarse as he stared at her. "Do you know how long I've been waiting for this?"

"No, tell me," she replied, bathing in the glow of what her heart told her was his love and adoration. She reached for his hand.

"Since I first saw you in Sweetheart Dreams, more than nine years ago."

His gaze thoroughly covered every silky inch of her skin. His mouth followed, with moist heat. She curled into him, her soft moans urging him on. Beneath the exquisite torture, Vanessa writhed on the bed in a haze of pleasure. When she could, she smoothed her fingers across the soft hair sprinkled across his molded chest and flat stomach. Her hands wandered restlessly along his toned body to caress the warm, polished smoothness of his rock-hard erection. The man had been seriously blessed. Her breath caught as he lovingly feasted on her breasts, his fingers moving deep within her. Her breath came in pants that ratcheted up to sighs as he moved down to tongue her navel. She curled her fingers into his soft, wiry hair.

"Give it to me, baby!" he growled.

Then he was kissing her intimately with a heat that caused her hips to rise up off the bed. Vanessa's high-pitched cry filled the room. She trembled and shook in the throes of a passionate release. Before she could catch her breath, he thrust a foil package into her hands. Ripping it open, she smoothed it on his impressive length. Then she was on the edge of the bed, welcoming Taye as he pushed into the slick moisture between her thighs. Sighing with pleasure, they undulated together, riding the waves of sensation. At the tumultuous peak, they gripped each other, trembling, shaking as they climaxed then fell back on the silken sheets, totally spent.

Taye gathered her close, his lips brushing her cheek. "Ten on the Richter scale," he pronounced, chucking softly in her ear. "That was everything I thought it would be. And it was just a sample of what I've got waiting for you. Are you down for it? Can you stand the heat?"

Vanessa trailed a finger along his chest. "I like to play with fire."

Starting over, they played on the bed. This was her time to have some fun, to spend some time with Taye. Tomorrow she'd worry about the future.

Chapter 19

The scent of jasmine and exotic flowers lingered in the air. In the distance, the rolling waves sprayed the sun-dappled beach. Vanessa pressed a kiss on Taye's lips, lifted his arm from her waist and slipped out of bed. He was in a deep sleep. Obviously his ordeal on the boat had affected him more than he thought.

Gathering her clothes and dressing quickly, she grabbed her shoes and eased out of the bedroom.

Mackenzie lingered in the hall outside her room. His eyes were hard as his gaze touched on the rumpled lace dress she'd worn the night before and the heels she cradled in one arm. "Did you sleep well?"

Staring hard at him from under her lashes, she shrugged. He knew damn well what she'd been doing with Taye. Inwardly, she cringed, knowing that she'd put herself in a no-man's land. Taye would be furious when he found out that she was an agent working for the DEA, and Renee was sure to rake her over the coals about ethical considerations and jeopardizing the assignment. She held herself straight. Given the chance, she knew she'd do it all over again. Life was full of chances and some only came around once.

Using her key, she opened the door to her room. Mackenzie followed her inside, barely able to contain his anger. "Was he worth it?"

"Yes." She kept the emotion out of her tone. Vanessa pulled fresh clothes from her open suitcase. She didn't feel like talking or defending herself.

He hovered, obviously angry and determined to chastise her. "You could blow the whole case."

"I haven't, so get off my back," she snapped. "I'll be meeting Annika and leaving for the pick up in half an hour." She stepped into her bathroom and started to close the door.

"Did you learn anything new?"

Drawing a breath, she told him what she'd heard about Taye and Jerrell being set up and about Taye's contact being killed in a Miami nightclub.

"Tough breaks," Mackenzie muttered.

"Yeah." Vanessa shut the door.

An hour later she and Annika were on a ferry to Freeport. Tourists filled the boat on two levels, anxious to shop and sightsee. Vanessa sat between Annika and a college student who chattered on about her classes and her boyfriend. Vanessa scanned the crowd. Thankfully, she didn't recognize anyone. As well as DEA agents, her gut warned her, Taye might follow her to make sure all went well with the pick up. But nothing and no one seemed out of place.

When they reached Nassau they climbed off the ferry with the others and took a taxi to the duty-free market. There, she and Annika wandered in and out of the shops. In the perfume shop, she picked brand-name scents for Taye, Mackenzie and Michelle. Aside from Annika and herself, there was only an old man in the store. At the front counter, he was going through the samples as if he had all the time in the world. Vanessa decided that if he was a DEA agent, his disguise was damn good, because he didn't appear capable of stopping anything.

Vanessa and Annika placed their packages on the counter and waited for the salesclerk to ring them up. After paying in cash, they accepted their bags. Vanessa gave hers a quick check. As she'd expected, when they received their bags, there were more wrapped packages inside than they'd actually purchased.

When she touched one to define the shape beneath the tissue paper, Annika urged her out of the store. "Girl, do you want to get yourself arrested or killed? Don't even touch that stuff," she admonished in a harsh whisper once they'd reached the safety of the crowd outside.

Acknowledging the warning, Vanessa gripped her bag by both handles and made her way down to the next shop. It was filled with straw goods and spices. This time there were three other people in the shop aside from her and Annika. No one even bothered to look up when Annika and Vanessa entered the shop.

She browsed, reading the names of the spices first. She must have earned an Academy Award for the way she went right past the Caribbean Mama Spice Mix. Instead she selected jerk chicken and pork seasoning and barbecue sauce.

This time when Vanessa received another bag full of extra packages, she didn't bother to check inside. She pretty much knew that the added packages contained the drugs. Fortunately, the combined weight of the packages wasn't too heavy.

Outside the shop a man in dark jeans and a white

T-shirt caught her attention before melting into the crowd. The beefy shape of his body and his hulking gait got her attention.

It was Jerrell.

Vanessa did a double take and her pulse started jumping. What was he doing here? And why hadn't someone from the DEA found a way to warn her? Jerrell was supposedly waiting for them at the villa.

"Cut that out!" Annika said sharply. "You're drawing attention to us. What are you looking at?"

Vanessa turned to face her. "I thought I saw Jerrell over there."

Fear flashed in Annika's eyes. She scanned the crowd, her jaw tightening. "Something's up." Her eyes assessed Vanessa and grew calculating. Her hand undid the snap on her purse and her hand slipped inside to where Vanessa had seen her stash her gun.

Watching her warily, Vanessa tensed.

"He could be checking on you. Is this a setup? They'll kill you if it is and you won't be the first. You're not DEA, are you?"

"No!" Vanessa rolled her eyes indignantly despite a rush of adrenaline. "I've got better things to do with my time. If something's gone wrong, you can't blame the shit on me. Next?"

Annika's expression grew more uncertain. "Jer-

rell here in the shops is bad news," she declared. "I
hope we're not in the middle of a raid."

"That's the last thing I need. You're supposed to
be showing *me* the ropes," Vanessa reminded her.
"When things seem wrong are we supposed to take
off like nothing's happened? Or are we supposed to
call somebody or something?"

"Unless we get a call from Jerrell, we finish
this," Annika said, some of the steel seeping back
into her tone.

"Okay. Want to get the last shop out of the way?"
Vanessa asked, her nerves jumping.

Annika nodded and tentatively led the way. Her
steps became more confident as they got closer to
the last stop.

Sudden shouting cut through the music and chat-
ter filling the area. Vanessa heard the disturbance before she saw it, then someone barreled through the
area, knocking people down, pushing over vendor
carts.

Stepping back, she caught her breath when she
saw that two uniformed police officers followed.
The runner moved with a grace and agility that
helped him elude capture for several moments.
Her eyes strained anxiously in an attempt to identify him. A glimpse of pecan-colored skin and a
long braid escaping a red scarf on his head al-

lowed Vanessa to breathe. He was no one she recognized.

The two uniformed cops and two more men collared the man down near the perfume shop and dragged him off.

"I've had more than my share of excitement for today," Annika muttered as they stepped into the last shop, which was full of souvenirs.

"Amen," Vanessa shot back. For a few moments, she'd been almost certain she was going to have to knock Annika out.

The final pick up went off without incident. Vanessa and Annika held their packages tightly as they sat in a taxi on the way back to the dock.

"It's not usually this nerve-racking," Annika explained, speaking low so only Vanessa could hear. "Things were crazy because you thought you saw Jerrell."

"I *did* see Jerrell," Vanessa insisted.

"Well, we're going to talk about it when we get back," Annika promised.

Both women were quiet on the ferry trip back. Vanessa cast covert glances at the other passengers but could not spot anyone who might be with the DEA, nor did she see Jerrell. She knew that Mackenzie had been ordered to stay out of the day's operation by his bosses.

Taye was out on the covered porch when they made it back to the villa. The visible relief on his face at the sight of her made Vanessa feel like a rat.

Inside, Jerrell was waiting in the great room. He was silent as Annika recounted their adventures on Nassau and seeing the man chased down by the local police. Nodding, Jerrell took it all in calmly. Apparently, Vanessa and Annika had been the last in the group of models to do pick ups. The other jobs had gone off without any unusual occurrences.

"Were you in the shops on Nassau?" Annika asked when it seemed that Jerrell wasn't going to bring it up. "Vanessa thought she saw you outside one of the shops."

Jerrell's head shot up. His penetrating gaze targeted Vanessa. "You're more observant than you look."

Vanessa kept her mouth shut. It seemed she was under suspicion again.

Jerrell faced Annika. "Caulfield asked some pointed questions that made me nervous, so I went through a couple of the pick up points to get a feel for what was going on. The place was crawling with cops. Until they chased down and collared that runner, I thought they were set up to take you two down." He gave Vanessa an apologetic glance. "We have to be careful who we trust, Vanessa. Our lives and our freedom depend on it."

Vanessa mounted the steps. One thing was certain. They didn't trust her.

The boat pulled away from the dock in a smooth, easy motion. They were headed back to Miami.

Taye sat in a deck chair behind Vanessa, staring out over the horizon. He hadn't said more than a few words to her since she'd left his room. Deciding not to push it, she stayed at the stern until the dock and the island became a tiny spot in the distance.

Afterward, she went inside to the main cabin, where several models were dancing to loud reggae music and amusing themselves with Jerrell, Mackenzie and some of the crew. Caulfield had already taken the plane back to Miami.

She sipped ginger ale and forced herself to circulate among the group. After the first pass, she settled on a couch with a window that looked out onto the water.

A red-and-white Coast Guard boat flying the United States flag came into view and progressed until it was close to the starboard bow of the boat. Through her window, Vanessa could actually see the faces of the crewmen on board. The room fell silent except for the music and a couple of the models who were chattering on about their assignments. The Coast Guard boat kept up with them, matching their speed for several minutes.

Vanessa began to wonder if the Coast Guard was planning on boarding their boat. It didn't make sense to her: she was almost certain that the boat she was on was still in international waters. Eventually, the Coast Guard boat moved on, but Vanessa had the sense that nearly every person in the room had felt the imminent threat.

Jerrell and a couple of the crew members casually stood and made their way back to one of the other cabins. Determined to follow and see what they were up to, Vanessa met Mackenzie's gaze. Hopefully he'd watch her back this time.

After a couple of minutes she slipped from the room and followed. Vanessa made it nearly all the way to the other end of the yacht before she found them in the storage area that sometimes doubled as extra sleeping space.

When she heard Jerrell's voice, she flattened herself against the wall. Ripping, rustling and packing sounds filled the air. Several minutes passed before she felt confident enough to risk a quick look. Vanessa stared, mesmerized, like a mouse within the sight of a deadly snake. Jerrell and one of the crew members were busy pouring white powder from a large plastic bag into one of the yacht's bumpers. The powder was clearly cocaine.

Vanessa thought back to the trip to Nassau where she and the other models did pick ups. Apparently Jerrell had made a pick up of his own. The appearance of the Coast Guard had obviously prompted him to find a better hiding place.

Stiffening at a sound in the space behind her, she swallowed a shriek. Someone grabbed her from behind and a beefy, calloused hand covered her mouth. Though she worked her elbows and tried to kick, she was carried forward into the room.

"Look what I found," a male voice announced proudly.

Jerrell and the other crewman that she recognized as Joe, stopped what they were doing. "Snooping around, huh?" Threat laced Jerrell's tone. "I never did quite trust you. What are you? A cop? Some kind of narc?"

Vanessa shook her head, frantic to get loose. When an arm came free she swung and caught her assailant, Stu, with a sharp elbow to the gut. Grunting, Stu loosened his hold. She rotated and rammed a fist into his nose. Her thoughts were racing as she anticipated their next move.

Jerrell and Joe rushed forward. A vicious front kick to the groin and Joe went down easily. But before Vanessa could regain her balance, Jerrell's hard fist caught her in the face and sent her reeling.

Vanessa blinked, slowly coming to, her vision clearing. She lay prone. Surely Jerrell hadn't knocked her out with one punch. Her jaw ached, and, to make matters worse, someone had stuffed a nasty rag into her mouth. She couldn't move her arms or legs.

"Hey, Sleeping Beauty." It was Jerrell's voice. Someone snickered in the background. "You know, I usually don't like my mules to sample the product, but you're a connoisseur. You can appreciate the good stuff, huh?"

Vanessa tried to shake her head. Sharp pain in her face and neck brought tears to her eyes. Her vision cleared a little, and fear gripped her. They were going to kill her.

Jerrell had some of the powder on a spoon. He waved it in her face. "If you've gotta go, this is the way to do it," he declared. "How long has it been, huh? You really think you're done with this stuff? You know, you never quite get over the rush."

Vanessa struggled frantically. The thick rope bit into her skin.

Jerrell grabbed her by the hair, tugging viciously and gripping it close to her scalp. Twisting her body, she racked her brain for a way out. Then it came to her.

To avoid breathing in, Vanessa held her breath. She'd been doing it from the time she was a kid and could hold out for several minutes. One of the crewmen palmed her breast and squeezed hard, his other hand closing on the belly-button ring. In pain, Vanessa grunted against the rag and drew a quick breath, and Jerrell was waiting.

The powder went up her nose with a harsh, burning sensation. The rush hit her like a train going full speed to hell. Shaking, she tried to swallow against the rag, suddenly feeling as if she could take on the world. The pain in her neck and jaw faded.

"Get away from her," Mackenzie ordered from the doorway. He'd drawn his gun.

Jerrell, Joe and Stu eyed him warily, sizing him up. They were slow to follow his orders.

"You," Mackenzie ordered, pointing to Stu. "Untie her, and take that rag out of her mouth."

The crewman drew a dirt-stained rag out of her mouth. Her stomach turned at the sight of it. She took deep breaths of fresh air as he slowly worked at the rope binding her hands behind her.

The other men eyed Mackenzie warily. In the tense silence Vanessa realized that the standoff between Mackenzie, Jerrell and his boys could not last for long.

Jerrell and Joe jumped Mackenzie, knocking the

gun from his hands. Maneuvering quickly, he punched and kicked both men karate-style.

Distracted by the fight, Stu stopped working on her bindings.

Vanessa looked for a way to free herself. Sitting up, Vanessa rotated her arms in the ropes and swung her arms and hands over her head. A mass of strong sailor's knots confronted her. She groaned in frustration.

"What's going on in here?" Taye stood in the doorway.

"Time to piss or get off the pot, bro," Jerrell called to him. "They're both narcs."

"Vanessa?" Taye's voice was rough with surprise and disbelief.

Lifting her bound hands, Vanessa appealed to Taye. If he was the man she thought he was, he'd help. "No, I'm not a narc, I swear—" Her voice faltered. "Help me, Taye. Jerrell drugged me and he's going to kill us."

Vanessa bit her lip in despair at the sight of Taye wavering in the doorway. She'd been wrong about him. She brought the rope to her teeth, determined to pull the knots out one by one.

At her side, Stu stood, apparently ready to join the fight. A hard, punching sound and a gasp close at hand captured her attention. Stu fell back to hit his head against the bulkhead. Dazed, he lay there, down for the count.

Gentle hands caught hers and began to loosen the knots in the rope with fast, efficient maneuvering. It was Taye. Vanessa couldn't speak. A tear ran down her cheek.

"I'm not going to lose everything I've worked for and spend the best part of my life in prison just because you've got the hots for this bitch," Jerrell declared.

At the statement, Vanessa and Taye looked up from the last knot and saw that while Mackenzie fought in a corner with Joe, Jerrell had managed to get to Mackenzie's gun. He was aiming it at Taye and there was no way Mackenzie could stop him. The air exploded.

Startled, Taye recoiled with a grunt of pain. A red circle bloomed just above his midsection and blood splattered Vanessa and Taye.

"Taye!" Vanessa shrieked.

Eyes closed, he fell back on the bed, breathing hard, gasping for breath and clutching his chest.

Vanessa stared down the barrel of the gun, throat working. Jerrell was aiming the gun at her. Taye was still holding her hand tight. Behind Jerrell, she saw that Mackenzie had knocked Joe unconscious and was inching toward Jerrell.

"Don't worry, you're going to die with him," Jerrell said, tightening his finger on the trigger.

In a risky split-second maneuver, Mackenzie tackled him, knocking him to the floor. Grunting, cursing and pummeling each other, they wrestled and fought over the gun.

Vanessa looked at Taye, pale beneath his rich coloring, and saw the blood pouring out of him through the hole in his chest. Thank God it wasn't his heart, but she was going to have to act fast. Bending over the rope on her legs, she worked the knots loose. She stood up shakily, her gaze riveted to Mackenzie and Jerrell, still struggling over the gun.

After a quick check of the doorway, she sprinted across the room. Stopping short of them, she tensed, lifted her right foot and brought it crashing down with a precision stomp-kick to Jerrell's head. His head snapped back on his neck and he went out.

Having retrieved the gun, Mackenzie stuffed it in his pants. "Good kick." He secured some of the rope that had been used on Vanessa and began to tie Jerrell's legs together.

Vanessa found more rope and helped tie up the others. Then she used her watch to call for backup and returned to Taye's side. The sight of blood dripping from the fingers of his hand holding his wound just above the midsection shook her. He was growing weak. As she prayed silently, she tore off the relatively clean bottom of her T-shirt and pressed it against the wound.

"Don't die on me," she whispered.

Mustering up a semblance of a smile, he muttered, "I ain't going nowhere."

"I know you called for backup, but we can't wait. I'm going to radio the Coast Guard, but we've got to get off this boat," Mackenzie said. There was a new urgency in his voice that stiffened her spine.

She glanced up at the empty corridor and guessed that the loud reggae music on the other side of the ship had covered the sound of the gunshots. "You think the others will take up the fight?"

"No. I need to show you something." He got up from the floor, moving slowly and with obvious effort. "I found the other coil of rope here," he said, pointing to an area behind a group of boxes. "And this—"

She felt herself shaking at the sight of the device attached to the wall close to the floor. She'd have recognized it even if she hadn't been instructed by Alan Burke on explosive devices. The cheap clock attached to a gray block of C-4 was clearly a bomb.

Chapter 20

"A bomb? Why?" Vanessa gasped.

Mackenzie shrugged. "I wondered why they didn't send some people back by plane and put others on a different boat. I heard one of the crew say that this boat belongs to Carouthers. He knows that Mila isn't dead. My guess is that this is the solution to all his problems. Everyone who can tie him to the drug operation is on board. And with Taye gone, the record business and recording studios are his."

Blotting her damp forehead on her forearm, Vanessa got down on her knees to examine the bomb from all angles. It seemed crude and simple, but she knew better than to proceed on an initial assumption. Besides, she knew that her overwhelming feeling of confidence was due to the cocaine. The best option was to get everyone the hell off the yacht and as far away as possible—but what if the lifeboats had been sabotaged?

She sent Mackenzie to check the lifeboats and round up the others while she tried to decide on the best course with the bomb. The clock indicated that they had twenty minutes. The wires coming out of the top were purple, orange and blue, but green, pink and yellow were also visible. What kind of wiring convention was it?

Her glance strayed to the end of the room where Taye was slumped against the wall, out cold. She swallowed hard and moved in closer to the bomb and got to work.

Mackenzie ran back with her purse and her cell phone. Only one of the lifeboats was usable, he reported. He'd already assisted the others in lowering it into the water and boarding it. They couldn't all fit in it, but help was on the way. There was room for one more.

She tried to convince Mackenzie to take the extra seat, but he refused to leave. And there was no way to lower Taye overboard in time and still deal with the bomb. Mackenzie released the boat and Vanessa dialed Alan.

Alan's voice filled her ear, at first cheerful but quickly turning worried. She was down to nine minutes. It took another minute to describe her situation and the bomb. Frayed nerves were making her antsy and the feelings of supreme confidence were fading. She felt the beginning of a dull ache in her jaw.

Alan accessed his database and even used the link to the Bomb Disablement Center at Sandia National Laboratories for information. Nothing in the extensive database applied to disarming the bomb.

Vanessa used the cell phone to send Alan a picture of the bomb. They were down to six minutes. Wiping beaded sweat off her upper lip, she met Mackenzie's gaze.

"If we get down to two minutes, we jump off the deck and swim for it," he said.

Vanessa didn't think she could live with herself if she let Taye or Mackenzie die.

Using a quick process of elimination that took into account the leads connected to the battery, the way the explosive was positioned and gut instinct, Alan told her to cut the orange wire. She'd more or less come to the same conclusion.

Armed with the nail clippers from her purse, she gritted her teeth and cut the lead. Nothing happened.

She allowed herself to breathe. Then she described the results to Alan.

Alan's voice held a tremor. "I don't know what to tell you," he confessed, "and there's no time to call for more help. We're going to have to guess."

She broke the news to Mackenzie. He stopped pacing the floor. "I'll do it," he said.

She checked the clock. Three minutes. "No. Take Taye to the open deck," she said. "You'll both have a better chance there."

She thought he was going to argue with her. He didn't. Sparing a glance at the men they'd been fighting, now tied up and struggling against their bonds on the floor, he used a fireman's carry to heft Taye onto his back.

Examining each wire, Vanessa went over the logic for cutting each one. There really wasn't any, but pink was the hottest color of wire remaining. Then she shook her fingers out. With a silent prayer, she leaned forward and cut the pink wire.

The countdown on the cheap clock stopped.

She'd done it! Ears ringing, she dropped forward to rest her forehead on her bent knees, her entire body trembling.

A totally new kind of euphoria took over as she stood and ran all the way to the open deck. Her face was wet with tears.

Mackenzie sat on the edge of the bow, poised to react to an explosion. He'd shielded Taye's prone figure with his. In the distance, a Coast Guard boat closed in on them, and the yacht's lifeboat floated several yards away on the other side of them. They were being rescued.

At the sight of her, Mackenzie jumped down to pull her into a bear hug. "You did it!" He swung her around, fairly dancing across the deck. "You did good, girl."

She dropped down to the deck beside Taye. He was unconscious and his hands were cold.

Vanessa saw the rest of the day from a remote view, as if in a dream. The Coast Guard rescued everyone. Afterward, they searched the ship and promptly took the entire group in for questioning and arrest. Taye and Jerrell were taken to the hospital under guard.

Under the guise of taking her aside for questioning, the Coast Guard debriefed Vanessa. She was formally thanked for her role in bringing down the gang. The cover story they agreed on involved her parents: their connections, money and good lawyers had gotten her off without charges.

The weird thing was that her parents—usually so distant—actually arrived in Miami, armed with the family lawyer, Derwood Jackson. They'd heard that Vanessa was among a group of people taken off a yacht with a bomb on it. Her mother cried effusively and hugged her a lot. Her father simply hugged her hard and told her that he didn't always agree with the things she chose to do, but he'd always loved her and been proud of her independent spirit.

This *had* to be a dream.

Her suddenly concerned and supportive parents even followed her to the hospital and sat with her while she hovered around Taye's bed in the Intensive Care Unit. The bullet had come dangerously close to his heart, but he'd already had surgery and was expected to recover. Beneath his normally rich brown coloring, he was still pale, but no longer bleeding.

"Vanessa, you're exhausted. Go home and get some sleep. You can come back in the morning after the anesthetic has worn off," her father chided gently.

"No. I'm not leaving until Taye wakes up and talks to me," Vanessa said. "I'll give you my keys and you and Mom can spend the night in my condo."

"No. I'm going to wait right here with you, honey," Vanessa's mother put in.

"I'm staying, too," her father said, easing down

into the chair on the other side of Vanessa. "I want you to know that we're here for you."

Mackenzie dropped by the hospital to check on Taye. Vanessa ignored her parents' speculative glances as she introduced them. She was certain that in their eyes, he would be a much better candidate for their daughter than Taye Rollins.

Drawing Vanessa aside, Mackenzie told her that based on the information they'd gained of Caulfield Carouthers's involvement in the drug ring and blackmail scheme, a team had already been sent out to search his home and bring him in for questioning. "He won't get away with it," Mackenzie promised. "Thanks to you."

"Thanks to both of us," she corrected, returning his friendly smile.

When Vanessa went in to see Taye again, his eyes opened. "We made it?"

"Yes." Vanessa swallowed hard. Those damn tears were back. She grabbed a couple of tissues from the stand and blotted her face.

"You must be my angel." His hand gripped hers tightly. "Kiss."

She leaned in to drop a kiss on his dry lips and stayed to rub her cheek against his, careful to avoid the razor stubble and the tubes and wires leading into him.

"Do you believe in love?" he whispered.

Vanessa nodded. "Yes."

"I think I'm in love with you."

She closed her eyes tight and burrowed her face deeper into the place where his head met the pillow. She was wetting both their faces.

"You don't cry much," he observed, his hand caressing her back. "Are you kicking me to the curb?"

Vanessa tensed. It was what she'd been advised to do. Her parents would no doubt be ecstatic, since Taye would have a hard time avoiding prison. But what did she want? She wanted Taye.

"Vanessa?" he prodded.

She felt the tension in him. "No, I'm not getting rid of you."

He released his breath on a sigh. "I'm not a hoodlum or a thug. I was blackmailed into looking the other way on some things. Vanessa, I do a lot of good—"

"I know that." She dropped another kiss on his lips, certain she felt some of his tension ease.

His eyes were shiny. "What about Caulfield?"

"They're searching his house and bringing him in for questioning. Jerrell was here in the hospital for a while, but now he's in jail along with the others. Taye, there was a bomb on the yacht."

His eyes widened. "A bomb?"

"Yes. We think Caulfield was trying to get rid of all of us."

He nodded. "It fits, especially when you consider the fire on my yacht. Am I going to jail?"

"I don't know," she said honestly. The prospect numbed her mind. "There's a cop outside your door. Maybe they'll find both tapes at Caulfield's home. Maybe you can use the Grand Caymans bank information to cut a deal."

On the way to her condo in the limousine her parents had rented, the events of the past couple of days were jumbled in her mind. She'd been through hell and wasn't quite clear of it yet. She had to do everything in her power to make sure Caulfield Carouthers paid for his crimes and that her work with the DEA remained secret. And she prayed she and Taye could be together.

Two months later in Montego Bay, Jamaica, Vanessa sat at the breakfast table on the deck, drinking coffee, eating fresh bananas and pineapple and reading a copy of the *Miami Sun*. The sounds of the sea rushing the shore provided a pleasant backdrop. Only yards away, the golden beach beckoned.

A smile lit her face when she read that Caulfield Carouthers's murder trial was scheduled to start. If that didn't stick, there were several more charges to go. She'd already had the satisfaction of seeing Jerrell go to prison for attempted murder and drug trafficking.

"Life is good," she murmured as she stood to stretch in the sun.

"You look like something I dreamed up."

Turning at the sound of the voice, she saw Taye in the doorway, dressed only in a pair of trunks. Her mouth watered at the sight of him. The scar on his chest was already beginning to fade.

Smiling, she opened her arms.

He went into them, his fingers curving around her hips to hook into her bikini bottoms. "I did dream you up," he murmured, his lips on hers, warm and caressing.

"I think we're both dreaming," she quipped, leading him down the steps and onto the beach. It had been hard waiting for Taye to recover from his wound and fight his way to guaranteed freedom. He'd had a good lawyer, two tapes found in Caulfield's safe, Caulfield's bank information, Mackenzie and Vanessa's testimony, and his own testimony at all the trials to help in the process.

Life was good. She had Taye, and her parents were being supportive for a change. They'd even given her a few suggestions for the new business she was starting in a couple of months, Star Showcase.

With the business, she would act as a liaison between clothing designers and movie stars, musicians, and other people in the public eye. The stars would gain the use of stylish clothing, a lot of it designed with them in mind, and the designers would get much-needed publicity. Vanessa would get a generous fee and be that much closer to personal independence.

A light wind tickled her face as they walked in the sun. Vanessa curled her toes in the sand. In a few days, she would return to New York to deal with her family, her studies and a detailed session with Renee. For now, she was determined to savor her victory.

Epilogue

Days later in New York, Vanessa entered Renee's private dining room for tea. Renee stood and hugged Vanessa hard. Then she regarded Vanessa affectionately. "I was concerned," she confessed, "and I'm glad it's over, but I always knew you could successfully complete that assignment. You're a lot stronger than you realize."

"Yes, I found that out the hard way," Vanessa confirmed. Renee was rarely this emotional.

Renee gestured her to a chair. "Is there really any other way to realize your strengths?"

Vanessa shook her head. "I guess not."

Renee poured tea into Vanessa's delicate cup and filled her own. "Just in case I haven't made myself clear, I am so proud of you Vanessa, and all that you accomplished on this assignment. I wish everyone could know what a hero you are, but you know that's not possible due to the nature of our work and the secrecy involved."

"I'm not in this organization for the glory or the fame," Vanessa said. "I took the assignment because I wanted to give something back, to help others, and I had to bring down Gena and Bianca's killers."

Renee lifted her cup of tea. "Here's to success."

"Here, here." Vanessa mirrored the gesture and carefully sipped the hot liquid.

"As a woman who's only recently gotten her family back, I know how happy you must be to have reached a new understanding with yours," Renee said. "What a bonus, hmmm?"

Vanessa stared into her tea and thought about the warm welcome home she'd just received from her parents. "I'm still feeling my way, but I'm not in the rut anymore."

Renee offered a plate of pastries. "And while we're talking about success, we've gotten another good lead on the Duke."

Vanessa selected a cheese pastry and bit into it.

"Caulfield Carouthers? Don't you think he's going to prison for attempted murder?"

"I certainly hope he goes to prison for everything he's done. Still, from what we've been able to gather, he's not the Duke."

"He's not?" Vanessa interrupted. "I don't believe it."

Renee regarded her steadily. "Believe it. Caulfield may be reprehensible, but he isn't the Duke."

"Then who is?" Vanessa blurted.

Renee set her cup down. "In the interest of preserving an ongoing mission, I can't say."

Vanessa shook her head. She'd been certain that Caulfield Carouthers was the Duke. He certainly fit the profile that had been developed.

"Let's talk about the mission you just completed," Renee prompted gently.

Shaking her head once more, Vanessa began to describe her first day on the assignment. An assignment she'd successfully completed, even if most people would only know her as a sexy model in a bikini, and not as a model spy.

*Turn the page for an exclusive excerpt from the
final book in the exciting*
THE IT GIRLS *miniseries
from Silhouette Bombshell.*
*BULLETPROOF PRINCESS
by Vicki Hinze
On sale February 2006
at your favorite retail outlet.*

Chloe's heart beat a little faster. This wasn't a social gathering. It was a professional briefing.

Renee Dalton-Sinclair didn't delay. "There's been a development in your current mission, Emma. The Governess has issued new orders, and they include you, Chloe."

The Governess was Renee's boss: a high-ranking individual positioned somewhere in the labyrinth of government, whose identity remained unknown even to Renee, much less to the Roses.

"Why isn't Tatiana here?" Emma asked, then sipped from her cup.

Tatiana Guttmann, a natural beauty, second-generation coffee heiress from Colombia, was Emma's current partner. People constantly underestimated Tatiana. She used her skills as a former model to mask the fact that she was very smart and an amazingly gifted financial analyst. In her social circle, no one would believe that she'd spent the past year working for Renee as a Gotham Rose agent, and that was an enormous asset as well as a necessity. Only secrecy allowed the Roses to function. Without it, they'd be stymied, completely unable to perform.

Renee hesitated only a second. "I'm afraid, my dears, Tatiana is the development—at least, in part."

"What do you mean?" Emma asked Renee.

"She's been dating one of the men from the escort service."

Emma's jaw dropped. "You've got to be kidding."

Chloe couldn't believe it, either. Tatiana was aggressively ambitious about two things: elevating her social standing, and remaining a darling in the press. Dating an outsider wouldn't further either goal, and she was all about furthering her goals.

Something had to have changed—and it well might have. Chloe wouldn't know the inside scoop since she basically ignored Tatiana—at least, she ignored her when they weren't in close proximity. If together, they were arguing.

"I wish I were kidding, but I'm not." Renee hid a frown behind her teacup. "Unfortunately, it's created a situation that the Governess finds discomfiting. So we're making some adjustments." Renee turned her royal-blue gaze on Chloe. "I've pulled Tatiana from the assignment, Chloe, and I'm inserting you to work with Emma."

Oh great. Chloe bet Tatiana was just going to love this. "What exactly is the assignment?"

"Based on multiple Intel reports, the Governess suspects the Duke is using an escort service that operates citywide as a front for a multitude of felonious activities."

"Renee." Chloe leaned forward, troubled by the direction of this conversation. "You do realize that about ninety-seven percent of the escort services in the entire state are prostitution rings."

"Actually, recent estimates are at ninety-four percent."

"Whatever," Chloe said, having no patience to quibble over a few percentage points. "Is the goal on this assignment to break up a prostitution ring?"

"More or less," Emma said. "And to identify the Duke, of course."

"Less now than more," Renee corrected Emma. "That's the other part of the development." She paused, delicately cleared her throat, and then went on. "We've had reports that some of the women hired by the service as escorts or models are being sold into white slavery and shipped out of the country."

"Good God." A chill shot up Chloe's spine and she gasped. "There is no low with that bastard. He'll do anything."

"We don't yet have irrefutable proof the Duke is involved," Renee reminded her.

"Why wouldn't he be? He's neck-deep in every other nasty nook and cranny." If only loosely, the Roses had already tied him to money laundering, bribery, drugs and a host of lesser, unsavory operations. If they could just catch the jerk, he'd rot in jail forever.

"Chloe has a valid point," Emma said, reaching for a raspberry tart. "Do we know how the service is choosing its victims?"

"Not in depth or with any degree of certainty, but an appearance pattern seems to be forming." Renee set down her steaming cup. "The three women we know are missing are all well-educated, well-spoken brunettes in their mid-twenties who can handle themselves in sophisticated settings. They're all beautiful, and they're all Russian."

"You can bet they're targeting vulnerable women," Emma said. "Ones new to the States, or ones without families who'll report them as missing."

"The Governess and her consultants fear that's true, and I agree with them," Renee said. "Intel has Dr. Morgan Cabot, its top profiler, working on this. She says the lone-victim target looks highly probable."

"What are Emma and I supposed to do?" Chloe's stomach suffered an uneasy pitch. "I know you don't expect us to make ourselves victims they'll snatch up and export to only God knows where. I'm a princess, after all."

Renee set her teacup down. "Actually I do."

Silhouette® BOMBSHELL™

THE IT GIRLS

Rich, fabulous...and dangerously underestimated.

They're heiresses with connections, glamour girls with the inside track.

And they're going undercover to fight high-society crime in high style.

Catch The It Girls in these six books by some of your favorite Bombshell authors:

THE GOLDEN GIRL by Erica Orloff, September 2005

FLAWLESS by Michele Hauf, October 2005

LETHALLY BLONDE by Nancy Bartholomew, November 2005

MS. LONGSHOT by Sylvie Kurtz, December 2005

A MODEL SPY by Natalie Dunbar, January 2006

BULLETPROOF PRINCESS by Vicki Hinze, February 2006

Available at your favorite retail outlet.

Where can a woman who has
spent her life obliging others truly
take time to rediscover herself?
In the Coconut Zone...

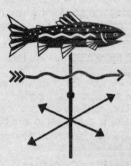

Off the Map

DORIEN KELLY

Available February 2006
TheNextNovel.com

COMING NEXT MONTH

#77 SOMETHING WICKED by Evelyn Vaughn
The Grail Keepers

Kate Trillo never had a burning desire to follow the family tradition of goddess worship and witchcraft. But walking in on her sister's murder changed all of that. When Kate's curse on the perpetrator went dangerously awry and hit his twin brother, she was forced to search Greece, Turkey and Italy for the family grail that would reverse the damage. Would she find her way back from the dark side…before she lost her way forever?

#78 BULLETPROOF PRINCESS by Vicki Hinze
The It Girls

For modern-day princess Chloe St. John, working undercover for the Gotham Rose spies provided a perfect chance to prove herself in the face of her mother's constant criticism. But nothing in Chloe's royal playbook prepared her to take down a criminal mastermind who anticipated her every move…and a fellow Rose who might be ratting her out to the enemy.

#79 THE MEDUSA GAME by Cindy Dees
The Medusa Project

As part of the all-female Medusa Special Forces team, photo intelligence analyst Isabella Torres was ready for anything. The latest assignment to protect an Olympic figure skater receiving death threats seemed routine—until the Medusas uncovered a larger terrorist plot to put the winter games on ice. Now with thousands of lives at stake, and seeming ski bum Gunnar Holt as partner in security liaison, could Isabella keep her cool?

#80 RADICAL CURE by Olivia Gates

Field surgeon Calista St. James thought she'd put her latest deadly rescue mission behind her—until a violent, mysterious illness started laying her colleagues low. Tracking the problem to a rogue lab in Colombia on a tip from her vigilante father, Calista *knew* she could beat the clock and find a cure…provided she could get her difficult boss Damian De Luna to play by her rules, and keep her feelings for him in check.…

SBCNM0106